MW01230560

Copyrignt © 2019 Richard Kroyer

Cover Art by

Jf.Vishna

See more at www.jfvishna.com

Beloved Everywhere poem by HAFIZ

This story is dedicated to my dear Co-pilot, Mr. Dillon, who shared with me how to access the silent space where wisdom resides.

Start seeing everything as God, but keep

it a secret.

Become like the man and woman who are

awestruck and nourished

listening to a golden nightingale sing

in a beautiful foreign language while God,

invisible to most, nests upon its tongue.

Hafiz, who can tell in this world that

when a dog runs up to you wagging, its

ecstatic tail, you lean over and whisper in

its ear,

"Beloved, I am so glad you are happy to

see me! Beloved, I am so glad, so very glad

you have come

1 Don't let reason into your heart

In his 47th year, Kyle was consumed with restlessness, and he thought, *Maybe I missed something significant in my life, and now I'm way off the path.* Every night was a repeat of the one before for Kyle. He would wake after a few hours of sleep drenched in sweat and consumed with anxiety. Although, he could sense something menacing, like a shift in the weather. He didn't know if something had occurred or would occur and became worn out and exasperated thinking about it. It seemed the reason for his anxiety always remained just out of reach, no matter how hard he searched. The darkness that overcame him clouded everything he did and seemed to follow him everywhere. Occasionally he could disregard it while conversing with someone or when immersed in some task. Still, he knew it wasn't a remedy because as soon as he was done, the darkness would return like stepping out a door surrounded by fog on a shadowy street. He thought his trouble sleeping and the stress around work might be causing much of his anxiety, but something else was creating anxiety too, something he couldn't quite put his finger on. Nothing seemed beyond that shroud of darkness, and the only thing he could think to do was set out walking like that old TV show about the Kung Fu expert. *Maybe traveling isn't the answer, but walking might give me the perspective I need right now.* The anxiety and restlessness had gotten to such an extreme that he thought his head would explode or he'd simply have a heart attack. Going back out into the world, while probably the last thing any 47-year-old "responsible" person thinks of doing, was his only solution. Uncovering the cause of his anxiety became the most important discovery for Kyle. He decided that if venturing into a scary and unfamiliar territory was required of him, that was precisely what he would do. The people in his age group probably think of retiring from life rather than creating something new.

Many of his friends believed they were doing Kyle a favor by trying to talk him out of this idea of going back out into the world. Eddie had been one of his best friends for years and was now the service manager for another airplane repair shop in town. Eddie stood a couple of inches over 6 feet, and his girth increased in recent years. Eddie was close to, if not a little more than, 200 pounds, so Eddie might have gotten used to dominating arguments with his size, though he tried to convince Kyle with logic. Conjuring a logical idea seemed nerve-wracking for Eddie, so he'd often rack his brain and return later with what he thought was even better logic for not "wandering around," as he put it. His thick black hair barely covered his fingers as he constantly tried to train it into a position it would never stay. Eddie seemed even more determined to train his hair as he struggled to find and employ the most compelling logic. He wanted nothing more than a "secure" future for himself and couldn't understand why Kyle wouldn't want the same. To secure stability for Kyle and a life of ease, Eddie thought Kyle was talking about; he brought up the old argument saying, "Why don't you sue that shop you work for? They owe you for that leg."

Kyle wrinkled his nose, "For what? They didn't do anything wrong." Gathering his thoughts for Eddie, he told him, "Maybe the worry I feel is because there was something I was supposed to do or be." Eddie ran his fingers through his hair again, this time stopping to grab a fistful and simulated pulling. Eddie mocked Kyle with a quote from a movie about a New York Italian boxer; "I coulda been sumbody. I coulda been a contenda."

Kyle smiled at the reference to a movie scene about missed opportunity and replied, "Maybe *I am* looking for something, but I feel I missed something important along the way. This may sound weird, but it seems something important was defined for me, and I never questioned or even looked at what was decided. I just feel like now I just have to start from scratch to see what I missed."

Eddie raised his eyebrows as he slowly shook his head. "Yeah, maybe you did miss something, but you still have a secure position at that shop if you don't go wandering around. You know that shop would never replace you. What could be so important to you that you'd leave and give that up? You know you're not 20 years old anymore. What is it? W*hat are* you looking *for*?" Eddie ran his fingers through his hair but made his scalp white by pressing so hard this time.

Shrugging, Kyle said, "I don't know. Maybe I'm not supposed to know."

"Now, what's *that* supposed to mean?" Eddie scrunched his eyebrows and leaned forward a bit, "Did something happen at work?"

Kyle shook his head, "No. Everything is fine there, but every day, for me, is identical to the one before. I don't feel like any day in the future might include some accomplishment. There's nothing that I'm doing differently or that I'm challenged to achieve. Maybe I am comfortable, but I feel my life has become absolutely trite."

Eddie rolled his eyes and sarcastically said, "Yeah! That's called a job." He turned to Kyle with a penetrating look. "This idea you have of wandering isn't going to that. When I was young, I had an idea to wander around, but thankfully my dad convinced me to refocus and not go wandering around." Eddie's hands came down on his knees with a slap, and he stood for emphasis, saying, "I have to pick my son up from football." Heading for the door, Eddie said over his shoulder, "I'll call you this evening, and maybe we can go out for a beer or something."

Most of Kyle's other friends mentioned his age as if that might be some watertight argument. They'd sometimes continue with, "Someone even half your age would know better than to just stroll off without a destination." Kyle could have become angry at these words, but he felt sorry for those who wouldn't support him. When his friends asked for a plan, he would shrug, and that shrug was always met with a blank stare. Some thought that by shrugging, he intended to take a spontaneous vacation, one person thought it would be a great adventure, but the rest thought he was just weird. Kyle had no mission to guide him, no plan to stick to, and nothing that even resembled an ending. His friends were not at all satisfied with the idea that his voyage was so loosely organized and maybe somehow beyond words. Initially, he tried to impart the sense that the journey might be too important for words and possibly beyond questioning. That statement would prompt more questions, so he'd just returned to shrugging.

Sometime the following week, Kyle wandered out to the edge of the airfield for his lunchtime stroll into the quiet away from the hangar and office where he works. He had looked out the window earlier to check how the weather might be. It seemed about perfect to him: low 70's and sunny. His lunchtime strolls are never a struggle, as the grass is always trimmed to about six inches. A slight buzzing sound started him scanning the sky. Kyle spotted a tiny speck of an aircraft way off in the distance, surrounded by an ocean of blue. He thought, *The pilot of that craft is probably aiming for this runway, but it'll be at least fifteen minutes before they get here.*

The sun warmed his back as he stood gazing at the speck in the sky. Maybe all that open space around the aircraft in the sky and the empty field surrounding him made him imagine he had a similar immense mental space to scrutinize that conversation he had with Eddie a few days ago. Kyle saw Eddie was making himself a little crazy while trying to devise some irrefutable argument against wandering. Kyle pondered how he might spare Eddie from creating further stress. *Traveling might give me the time and space I need and also spare Eddie from his crazy-making routine.*

Kyle thought about all his years of being an aircraft mechanic that he might have to give up. He recalled replacing a pair of magnetos on a small airplane years before when he was fresh out of aviation maintenance school. In one of his classes, he learned that an aircraft keeps the spark simple and separate from the rest of the electrical system for safety, so the engine will keep going if part of the electrical system fails.

Kyle was excited to be working as a mechanic at a local flight school as he pushed his enormous red toolbox out to the waiting green and white aircraft to start work on his first airplane. He approached the task the lead mechanic had given him, emboldened by all the information he'd been taught about aircraft in his years of aviation school. The lead had told him, "I appreciate your attention to even the smallest detail. I can't imagine how it must be in your head with all those thoughts always bouncing around, but good aircraft mechanics are sometimes hard to find, and I know I can always rely on you to ponder every possibility."

Kyle also thought of the romance of aviation that he'd miss—being called upon to perform some critical task on aircraft professionally placed Kyle in the middle of the romantic story of aviation history that he might no longer be a part of.

Gazing dreamily off into the blue and then renewing his focus on the tiny speck, Kyle reached a firm conclusion. *I know it's up to me, and I'm the only one who can decide if a journey is right for me. I can't imagine this life revealing anything significant for me, so I'm gonna journey to discover something new.*

Kyle smiled as he remembered an old friend saying, "Your continual thinking is like a rocket ship endlessly orbiting some planet with no way to land." Kyle interrupted, asking, "But what if it's a really important thought?" They cautioned, "No matter how unique a thought seems, the rocket ship will still make the same useless orbits. Sometimes, the best cure for chronic thinking is taking a little breather." Pointing at Kyle, "And don't let reason into your heart."

Kyle cocked his head to the side, saying, "Huh?"

They explained, "Sometimes it's challenging for people to pay more attention to the wisdom in their hearts than the stuff they may have heard. It seems they often mistake those reasonable thoughts floating around in their head for the pure wisdom they already have, so a lot of the things you hear may seem wise, but you don't want to let those reasonable thoughts eclipse your wisdom."

His smile faded as he vaguely recalled something else said. *It seemed like it was also about thought, kinda like 'Whatever you think becomes true for you.' Like if you see others as unfriendly or untrustworthy, they will be.* He gently shook his head and thought, But I do understand w*andering around could fuel my rocket ship for a long time.* Kyle's shoulders slumped slightly as he dejectedly imagined his rocket ship *endlessly* orbiting. *Maybe I do need to take a breather and stop thinking so much.*

Kyle quit his job the day he visited the camping store to buy a backpack, some good walking shoes, and other things he thought he might need. While immensely significant for some of his friends, quitting his job gave Kyle a fleeting feeling of peace as it was his first tangible indication that he was moving along to find a new and maybe critical path. That feeling of peace was soon replaced with alarm. *I've chosen this path, and right or wrong, I'm going, but what if my friends were right? Yesterday was all just me talking, but now, I'm committed to traveling.*

He wandered around the camping store on their grey carpet for a while, fascinated by all the fancy gadgets in their vibrant colors. Kyle was particularly attracted to a big green backpack hanging with all the other packs. Kyle couldn't even recall having slept on the floor, let alone camping; smiling at that thought, he wandered across the store to browse the sleeping bags. Kyle saw a collection of wooden hiking sticks on the way to the counter with the green backpack and his heap of new gear. He certainly didn't need one, but he tried one for size. The staff's feel in his hand seemed to assure him and add a commitment to his journey, so Kyle placed it with his pile of new gear. The hiking staff would be in constant use on his journey as he planned to walk, as he wouldn't ask for a ride. Kyle thought *I'd accept if someone offered a lift, but until that offer, I'll just walk. If I focus on hitching a ride, I might miss something I'm supposed to see along the way.*

About two weeks later, Kyle started walking south out of the city where he'd lived most of his life.

Kyle felt his foot contact the ground as he walked along the road, making a unique sound. Kyle's thoughts seemed to be saturated by that feeling and sound. Still, occasionally he'd think back to his group of friends and how they tried to dissuade him from this trip: Kyle smirked at the thought of his friends' lack of support. He recalled Juan's words again, "You can't let reason into your heart." It gave him more confidence in his choice as he repeated the phrase to himself, and then his thoughts drifted back to the feel and the sound his footfall made when his shoes contacted the ground. He decided it was kind of a subtle clip-clop sound. His left shoe would make a slightly higher pitch sound than his right. The difference was almost imperceptible, but Kyle noticed and was drawn further into the sound as hours of every day he spent listening to his shoes contacting the pavement. Kyle was so tuned into the sound that even a change in the pavement color would signal a slight difference in the pitch of the clip-clop sound.

Kyle stopped early that first evening and discovered that setting up his camping gear was surprisingly easy. He had worried that he had no experience and might not even know up from down when assembling his camp. By the time everything was set up, it was getting just a little dark, so Kyle put his headlamp on to find his journal and climbed into his tent. Once inside his tent, he felt safe in the cocoon of his new sleeping bag, with his new headlight shining on a blank page of his journal. Everything seemed to have the feeling of adventure and newness.

My friends tried to talk me out of going on any excursion, and instead of saying, "See how high you can fly and tell me what you discover," I heard all about how people fail. I wonder if my friends actually believe there's an age limit to discovery. I realize how old I am and how it might have been odd to them that I couldn't say what the destination was or even why I was going, but if I hadn't taken that first step to journey, I could have changed my mind and lost all faith in myself. I now see how Eddie was possibly concerned about my well-being, but I think the rest were more concerned with something that might make them question their views. I assumed my friends would have words to inspire and motivate me, but I see that was just my fantasy. They probably didn't want me to forfeit the safety I had already secured. I remember as a rebellious young man; I loved choosing an obscure and uncertain path. I remember feeling like a bold adventurer who didn't require supportive friends, but at this moment, I don't feel at all bold. That was probably twenty-five years ago, and now I feel lonely and scared. Lonely because that group of people I call friends would probably not welcome me back, and scared because I've lost the identity that I had. It may not have been authentic, but that identity was all I had. Maybe I allowed my friends to define the borders of my identity, but it surprised me that when I went to look, they all became angry. I'd like to see who I authentically am, and I'd like to feel that

boldness again, like when I was that rebellious youth that wouldn't even consider letting reason interfere with going on a journey, but that was more than twenty years ago now I don't feel so adventurous.

I know I'm lost in life, but I'm trying to find my way, and I wish my friends would've supported that search. I may be blind and lost, but I'd still be lost even if I found a familiar sound to guide me, like a friendly voice. Am I like a lost, blind man tapping my cane against objects, hoping for a familiar sound to give me some direction? I remember Eddie asking me, "What is it? What're you looking for?" I couldn't answer because I didn't know then, and I don't know now. Maybe I am blind, but I know a blind person must be willing to venture forth and risk discomfort even to find a simple cup of water. I think that's real courage!

I wonder whether the blind man feels totally isolated and alone like I do today. Even though I may feel isolated and somewhat timid, I must continue this journey and hope some significance will be revealed to me.

Kyle had read a book about haiku poetry and tried composing one.

go confidently

discover forgotten truths

embrace what you find

As Kyle walked, he'd be lulled into a sort of trance by that subtle clip-clop sound. Kyle passed a sign that pointed to a path in the forest and vaguely wondered how the sound of his footfall would be different on the hard-packed dirt of that trail. As it seemed to be headed to the west, he ignored the trail going away from his intended direction. A few hundred yards later, though, he noticed the path winding its way next to him through the trees. He kept peeking longingly at the trail in the forest and, after a few minutes, looking again at the forest trail, *I guess I feel a little timid, simply leaving this road to travel that trail, but I can't say precisely what I'm out here to discover and what is really me. Maybe I should just march over there and*

11

see. And with that steadfast determination, Kyle trekked confidently through the brush to travel the trail.

Kyle was in complete wonderment at the extreme silence around him and, after a few hours, couldn't even remember his reluctance to leave the highway. He looked around at the peaceful, empty forest but was still a bit anxious. Kyle remembered hearing that maybe peace and wisdom could be right around the corner if you're anxious. *It seems like a person might have to struggle a bit to make wisdom chief in the mind.*

Kyle heard a faint click through the trees and stopped to listen. Hearing nothing but the whisper of the breeze in the branches, he continued walking. As soon as he took a few steps, he heard a similar click, stopped again, and tilted his head to listen again. The sound seemed to be coming from farther along the trail, and Kyle was slightly panicked. The trail made a slight bend around a tree and then disappeared behind some rocks so that he couldn't see, and he even glanced nervously over his shoulder as if that soft click could be sneaking up behind him through the shadows. Kyle hesitantly wandered forward along the trail with that faint click reaching him every once in a while, but as soon as he reached the rocks, he could see the sound was coming from a camera that was held by someone looking up the trunk of a tree.

2 Sometimes, you have to take a step back

Kyle called out a hello so as not to sneak up behind the photographer.

The photographer turned and waved, calling, "Hello."

When Kyle walked closer, he said, "Hey, I'm Kyle."

The photographer said, "I'm John. It's great to meet you!" Nodding at Kyle's gear, "I've done some traveling, and I've often wondered how the other person might experience the road?"

Kyle scrunched his brow and pondered this idea. "What do you mean by experience?"

"Like, how do you feel about being on the road, or maybe what are you discovering?"

After a moment, Kyle's face lit up. "Aah! I think I know what you mean. The hardest thing for me to do was to walk out on the life I'd built. My friends didn't support me walking out, but I somehow knew I had to travel." Kyle went on to explain more. "That first step was tough for me to take by myself if you know what I mean?" John nodded while Kyle was describing his feelings about travel, but John's phone interrupted as it rang.

Kyle could hear both sides of the conversation because John had the volume turned up on his phone. John told the caller that he was about done taking pictures for the day, so she told John about the spaghetti someone named Amanda had requested. John said, "That sounds great. I'll be about twenty minutes, and I'm bringing a friend I found in the woods." John nodded and hung up.

John said, "We'd love to have dinner with you. Follow me back to my house, so we can keep talking."

"Dinner would be awesome, thanks." Kyle pointed at the tree and asked, "What were you taking a picture of?"

John explained as they walked up the trail, and soon, some houses appeared through the trees. They approached one, and a little girl opened the door. She looked up at Kyle and said, "Hi." John swept her up in his arms, saying, "I heard you ordered a great dinner for us." Turning to Kyle, "This is Amanda. My wife Mary and her daughter Elaine are around here somewhere. You're gonna stay with us tonight. We have a spare bedroom that hasn't been used in weeks. You can put your pack in there."

"That's very cool. Can I do anything to help with dinner?"

John said, "Nope." While pointing to the couch with his chin, "Just make yourself comfortable."

When the pasta was done, all five assembled in the kitchen to spoon sauce over the spaghetti on their plates. Mary asked everybody to grab a couple of slices of garlic bread on the way to the table. John asked Amanda, "Do you want me to help you spoon sauce?" Amanda gave John a look for an answer and bobbed her head slightly. Mary started to pour some red wine into the four glasses on the table, but Elaine waved it off, saying, "I'm going out later with some friends."

After dinner, John helped Amanda make her way to bed, and Elaine made her way to the club, leaving John, Mary, and Kyle with the rest of the wine.

Mary pointed to the living room and smiled, saying, "Let's take our glasses; we'd probably be more comfortable on the couch."

As they moved over to the living room, Mary looked toward Kyle. "John told me something about having to make a hard choice about traveling. Can you tell me about it?"

Kyle nodded, "Sure." Pausing to take a sip of wine. "I felt like I was on a path that wouldn't ever challenge me. I'd spent years studying aviation maintenance, and it was challenging to contemplate trading that for something unknown, but I felt capable of more, so I knew I had to. Travel seems to reorder things."

Mary wrinkled her brow. "What do you mean, reorder?"

Kyle said, "To me, reordering just means discovering the fundamental importance of things that I think about or do. Back home, I couldn't really see what things were crucial, so I had to travel and hope the critical things became more important in my mind."

Mary nodded slightly and said, "I think I get what you mean. Sometimes I get a bit out of sorts at the office where I work and can't decide what's critical, so I take a bit of a walk."

Kyle said, "Absolutely. Sometimes it's hard to know what's critical, and a bit of a walk helps."

When he was done, John asked, "So that's what you meant by the difficult choice you had to make to travel? Yeah, I think travel has helped me a bunch."

Pointing at some pictures of John on the wall, "I see that. Is that a surfboard next to you in that photo?"

John said, "Yeah. That's the board I have downstairs. I think traveling has given me the space to relax and breathe. Some find the breath in breathing, and others," pointing his thumb at himself, "maybe find the breath in the event. Neither is right or better, but if a person finds their breath in some activity, like surfing, natural breathing seems to happen."

Shifting to look over his shoulder at the bunch of photos on the wall, John said, "I've been to a few places, but I think my current opinion of life came to me while in Costa Rica. Maybe it doesn't have anything to do with Costa Rica. Still, the culture down there is very different than what we're used to seeing in the U.S. It seems that journey put certain things in perspective for me. It's like taking a step back. Doing something at a completely different pace or an entirely new way put me in a great space to examine what's important. I understood that if wisdom equals the inward expression of value, then trying to make it an outward expression, or turn it into some kind of gain, might be the same as moving through the world artlessly."

It hurt Kyle's head trying to follow all that, so he asked John to slow down. John nodded and pointed skyward, saying, "Okay, let's assume the big guy is going to have a chat with you, and you're really specific about what you think is going wrong in your life. What do you imagine GOD might say in response? Do you think GOD would tell you, *Your problem is you're not making enough money?*" John explained, "Striving to make more money might be that outward expression I talked about. Or do you think GOD might tell you something like, *Maybe this is an opportunity to grow your wisdom?*" John said, "Growing your wisdom would be that inward expression I talked about." John nodded and continued, "It's not hard to grow your wisdom, but many people want to take that wisdom to a bank and convert it into cash, which doesn't work at all. Those same people believe that growing wisdom is just a useless waste of time." John pointed a finger at his chest, saying, "The expansion of my wisdom is probably the most important thing I can do for myself and mankind."

Kyle nodded and smiled. Pointing at John, Kyle said, "Now, that makes sense. Trading wisdom for money sounds like a terrible idea." Looking back at the photo of John on the beach, he said, "Surfing seems really powerful, but I can't swim too good."

John nodded toward the bookshelf. "Surfing is only one way. There are many different ways, and many masters have written about the attainment of wisdom through the years."

Kyle got up and wandered over toward the bunch of books, and as he was looking through the book collection, a few caught his eye. Looking over his shoulder, he asked John, "Would you like to trade? I just finished reading the book in my pack, and I'm ready for something new."

"Sure!" John nodded, saying, "This is perfect timing; I'm looking for something new to read, too."

Kyle shelved his book, and his fingers floated over to a book with some Eastern calligraphy. John noticed the book in Kyle's hand and said, "That's a great one, and he was a local author too."

Pulling it out and holding the book for John to see, Kyle said, "I'll read this one, then." Turning back to Mary on the couch, "That spaghetti was fantastic, and I'm gonna do a little reading before bed, so I'll see you in the morning."

Pointing at the spare room, Mary said, "Great. We'll see you in the morning; sleep well. We usually do coffee about six."

Kyle pulled out his sleeping bag to put on the bed and started to read his new book. However, he was preoccupied with a thought and had to put the book down a few moments later. *The image keeps replaying in my head of John pointing to his chest and affirming that the most significant thing he could do for the world would be the expansion of his wisdom. At first, I thought he was being selfish, but now I can't think how he might benefit from the attainment of wisdom. His journey seems like what I remember of a knight in shining armor, where there was only hardship and no hope of reward in the stories. I think that's very courageous, and from this moment forward, I'll seek wisdom, too.*

Kyle reached over to his backpack to pull his journal out.

I think attaining wisdom is probably the most important thing I could do too. I was totally fascinated by John's story about attainment of wisdom. I could almost visualize myself in that role, but the attainment of wisdom seems like an immense task. I wouldn't even know where to start.

John said many people try to convert their wisdom into cash, and I'll definitely try not to do that! It seems some people only value what they see as valuable, maybe like trying to show off their wisdom to another. It seems that trying to convince someone of some wisdom you gained might be deemed a sort of conversion, like when John was talking about taking wisdom to the bank. I wonder, if a person chooses not to share their wisdom for some reason, might they be considered unwise? Maybe in trying to convince another of some path to wisdom, wisdom is lost and forever changed into nonsense that sounds like gibberish. That's perhaps what John meant by moving through the world artlessly. It seems that hoping for a reward might be like trading wisdom, and the opposite of that would be like seeking to be planless or striving to find non-meaning.

Kyle let that thought sink in a bit and then shrugged as he shook his head, *That makes no sense.*

Kyle remembered standing in the sunny field next to the runway a few weeks earlier and recalled the immense mental space he felt while gazing at that aircraft. As he reminisced about that feeling of peace, an image of a rocket ship replaced the aircraft, and a disquieting feeling took over. Kyle decided to write a haiku about wisdom.

gargantuan task

the attainment of wisdom

strive for purposeless

The following morning John asked about Kyles' intended direction and got the subtle shrug in return. John nodded knowingly, saying, "Sometimes we have to take a step back to see the path more clearly."

John continued, "I've got a friend visiting from Belize in about a week, so you're welcome to that spare room until then. Hang out. We'd love more time to chat."

Kyle brightened and said, "That would be great! I'll probably have a great time looking around and doing some day hikes. Can I read some more of your other books while I'm in town?"

"Absolutely. Grab a few books."

Kyle spent the next few days relaxing around John and Mary's home and reading as many of John's books as possible. John interrupted his reading one day, pointing at the book he was reading. "I love the way that author writes. He talks about discovering the fact that we are the thing we seek."

Kyle raised one eyebrow. "How do you mean?"

John nodded at the book, "I think the author is pointing to the fact that all the searching we do is probably unnecessary because we already are the thing we search for like we might go in search of high-mindedness when we had it all along." John raised his eyebrows as he shrugged, taking a deep breath. "But sometimes we have to go in search of that very understanding."

Kyle shook his head gently in disbelief. "I don't understand that at all. How does somebody not know they don't need to journey to find something."

John shook his head gently, saying, "I'm not sure how all that works; I just see that relaxing and taking a step back are necessary."

Kyle's eyes wandered across the ceiling while he contemplated. His gaze finally reconnected with John. "I don't think I'm even close to understanding that idea."

"Conceptualizing of an idea is not important at all, but it seems that taking a step back may just lead to the understanding of why stepping back is essential. "

The idea that we don't need to search for anything doesn't seem very intelligent to me, but maybe I just don't understand what John means. I've committed to going on this journey.

That night, Kyle had another thought about his journey.

John said something the other day that I've been thinking over. He said, 'Sometimes you must take a step back to see the path more clearly.' I don't know why I felt I couldn't be on a path because I didn't have a destination, and maybe taking a step back would give my journey a meaning I feel it needs. I wonder if that understanding and statement was all I needed from my friends. It seems like a massive contradiction that someone doesn't need to journey to find meaning for their journey. I can't even imagine what John was talking about, and if I'd shared that idea with Eddie, I think his head would have exploded. I guess I would really like some purpose to my journey because sometimes it seems necessary.

target-less journey

man desires destination

meaning for journey

A few days later, Kyle told John he would continue walking south the next morning.

John nodded. "I know you'll have a safe journey."

As John and Mary came down the stairs with Amanda in the morning, Kyle told them, "Goodbye, you guys. I don't know how to say thanks for taking me in. I learned lots, and it was just a really cool visit."

Mary said, "It was great having you here, and we should thank you." Nodding towards the house, she added with a smile, "You know where we are, so drop in anytime. We'd love to have you."

3 Breath as grace

A few days over the California border, while listening to this clip-clop sound of his footfall, Kyle thought he also heard a rustling on the side of the road that startled him back to his whereabouts. *Maybe the rustling sound is a mountain lion, a bear, or some other creature that would tear me to pieces just for being in their terrain.* Looking around, Kyle let fear sink into his every pore as he wondered who would even find him out here as only one friend knew of his general whereabouts, and she disapproved of this plan of just walking out on everything. *I don't want to end up as just a pile of unidentifiable bloody bones and clothes off the side of some road in northern California.*

Kyle had read scary accounts of big cats attacking hikers and leaving chewed-up remains. In one article, the author claimed that the first sound you'd hear might be the cat's claws scraping on your skull. He shifted his pack to get ready to do his clip-clop run up the road, as the rustling turned into a crunching sound when the animal got nearer. He tried to remember what to do when attacked by a bear or cat. *Was it run if it's a cat: or was that for the bear? Was there something about standing your ground? I think there was something about falling to the ground and wrapping your hands around your neck for protection, but I can't remember what that article said to do, and all I have to defend myself is this wooden walking stick.* Kyle stopped to look back up the road as there was only an empty highway in front of him. He saw no dwellings out here, just hills on one side of the road and a cliff watching over the Pacific Ocean on the other. Kyle glanced up and down the road wishing for a car but found he was alone. He could see the leaves above the animal move as it got closer to the road. Just as he was about to bolt, a dog emerged from the bushes and casually fell into step with Kyle as if they'd been together for years.

Kyle let out a relaxed exhale and noticed he had been holding his breath, thinking that some vicious creature was out to get him. *This dog doesn't even look a bit wild, and that situation seemed totally anticlimactic.* Kyle felt slightly let down as he breathed long and slow. Smiling as he gazed down at the dog, he recalled many times in his life when he mistakenly denied himself the gift of oxygen. Pondering the intelligence of blocking the flow of breath, he noticed the dog had no collar. It looked so natural, matching his stride, that the thought never crossed his mind that this wasn't exactly where this dog belonged. As further confirmation that this dog ought to be here, as he looked back at his footprints, there were now 6.

Kyle thought, *Maybe this dog is just lost, but I wonder if she had to take that first step, like me, and just walk out on some life even if it was kinda comfortable. Maybe this dog knew it had to journey to discover some missing piece of its life.* Kyle shook his head, musing on the theatrical thought of a dog having a journey to discover a purpose. *That's just nonsense, he thought. This is simply a lost dog that I happened to find; it's just a dog, and it can't have a purpose.* With that thought, he reached down to pet this stray and discovered it was a she.

This dog looks like the pictures of Australian cattle dogs I saw in books: Kelpie was the breed mentioned many times. Though I can't imagine a dog serving any useful purpose on my journey, it looks like this one is coming along, so I'll probably have to name it. The name that came to him first was Dingo, and Kyle tried it out. The dog perked her ears and turned to look at him. Kyle thought maybe the name just rhymed with her old name. The idea that this dog was named anything like Dingo was just whacky. He sang a whacky song to his fellow traveler in response to that notion. The old song he remembered from childhood was a nursery rhyme about a man and a dog named Bingo.

So he sang: **B-I-N-G-O...B-I-N-G-O...B-I-N-G-O,** and **Dingo** was her name **O!** Dingo cocked her head every time he sang her new name.

Kyle could hear a car approaching through the verses of the song he sang to Dingo and wondered with a bit of frustration, *Where was that car a few minutes ago when I was afraid for my life?* Turning to look over his shoulder, he saw a gray, newish SUV driven by a girl. The car pulled over, and the girl emerged to ask, "Can I give you two a lift?"

Once Lucy had Dingo and Kyle loaded in her car, she continued driving south along the coast. After speaking with Kyle for a few minutes, she revealed that "Dogs are fantastic, but I was guided to stop because I knew there'd be some sort of exchange between us. I've learned not to second guess any guidance I receive. Maybe you and Dingo would consider staying with my wife and me for a few days. We have lots of space and would love to have you stop over."

Kyle felt slightly disoriented by all the latest happenings but thought this might be a delightful resting spot and, looking out at the Pacific, said, "That'd be great! If you're sure, it's no bother?" Kyle glanced briefly at Dingo, napping in the back next to his pack. Lucy smiled, saying, "Not at all! This will be awesome, and Stella loves the company."

The ride was another hour, during which Kyle learned that Lucy had been teaching Yoga at her studio in town and exploring Yogic philosophy for 10 or 15 years. She was coming from a friend's new Yoga studio up north, where she was helping instruct for a few days. Lucy and Stella have been married for almost eight years, and Stella has been a carpenter for about as long and works mainly around the small town where they live.

When the conversation died down, Kyle alluded to holding his breath before seeing Dingo appear. Lucy said, "In Yoga, the observance of breath is called pranayama. Sometimes the breath would be gently withheld so that the breath could be observed better, but what you're describing is more of an involuntary action. Can I show you a simple Yogic breathing exercise with a slight retention? It's an alternate nostril breathing called Nadi-Shodhana where you use your ring finger and thumb to gently close the nostril it hovers over." Lucy turned and smiled at Kyle, saying, "You'd usually close your eyes, but since I'm driving, I probably won't." She showed Kyle all the other steps saying, "It goes like this. Start by taking a full inhale. Close your right nostril with your thumb and exhale for a slow count of six. Gently hold the breath out for another slow count of six, then inhale through the left nostril for that same count. Hold the breath in for that count of six while switching nostrils by closing your left nostril with your ring finger, then exhale for a slow count of six through your right nostril. Gently hold your breath out for that slow count of six. Inhale through the right nostril for the six-count. Gently hold your breath in for the count of six while you switch to the other nostril and keep that cycle going. That can help with awareness around your breathing."

Lucy talked about the postures in Yoga, saying, "I always make breath the focus in my classes. The physical form is irrelevant if the breathing is at all disturbed. Many focus on the form, disregarding the flow of breath. While that can lead to a willowy physical form, true grace is shown through the individuals' breath." Shifting her surveillance off the road temporarily to look at Kyle, "An unobstructed inhale followed by a full exhale is not something we usually continue doing after childhood. Most of us learned to restrict a portion of our breathing somewhere along our path of life. It's not important why we stopped; it may have been a physical injury, repeatedly assuming a certain posture that might obstruct airflow or some mental state we acquired. Whatever it was, we can learn to breathe again and," nodding her head, "breathing fully in any situation allows your full grace to flow."

Lucy glanced over her shoulder at Dingo and then continued. "The definition of inspiration is simply the taking in of air, but some outside element can inspire you, or you can light on some new understanding that might bring you back to the breath, so when you hear somebody say the word inspired, you can think of a person being in-spirit. I think being in spirit would always include relaxed breathing."

Tapping the steering wheel excitedly with her index finger, Lucy added, "Our revelation may be equivalent to the inhale, and what we do out in the world might correspond to our exhalation." Laughingly she added, "But all philosophy aside, breathing is just a good idea." Kyle laughed, too, and nodded in agreement.

When they pulled into the drive, Kyle felt like he was traveling with a close friend. He went to the back hatch to let the now awake Dingo out. Stella came out to greet the whole party. She hugged Lucy; she sank her fingers into Dingo's fur and welcomed Kyle with a huge smile. Kyle noticed the house shared by Stella and Lucy was just a few hundred yards from the ocean, so he and Dingo would probably be down there often.

Kyle and Dingo went single file through the front door after Lucy and Stella. Stella pointed out the house's features to Kyle when they were all inside. "I had the house gutted after we bought it, and then I built it back just the way we wanted. Many of the modifications we made are to make this house more appealing to us, but they'll be functional for the following folks that live here. Kyle nodded and could feel the house almost embracing his admiration.

After putting his green backpack in the living room corner, Kyle excused himself and went with Dingo down toward the beach. Dingo followed Kyle down the few stairs from the house and past Lucy's car to the footpath leading them to the ocean. Kyle stopped as the footpath reached the sand and looked left and right down this half-mile stretch of beach. Both ends were blocked by boulders that had rolled down from the cliff, making a secluded and private beach. Dingo pushed passed Kyle, obviously anxious to reach the ocean. Kyle watched her jog down the beach as he sank into thought.

Dingo sniffed at the water as if investigating the ocean for the first time. Kyle pondered, holding his breath again. Kyle continued to question every idea he'd come up with about stopping his breathing sometimes and thought, *If I wanted to listen very deeply to something, it would make sense to withhold my breath. Still, other times I'd hold my breath that would make zero sense, like making a cup of tea.* No clear answer came, so he did some Nadi-Shodhana and felt immediately more connected to his breathing and the breeze on his face. Kyle decided always to breathe first and calculate after. With the confidence he didn't feel, he assured himself *I could accept any consequence from that decision.* As the sun was sinking into the sea, he turned to go back to the house. Dingo immediately turned to follow Kyle.

Dingo entered the house and was soon snoring into Kyle's jacket that he'd put in the corner for her. Lucy had made sushi with vegetables from their garden, and after sharing a relaxing evening meal, Lucy pointed at Dingo, saying, "You may have trouble getting her outside, but a great trail goes to the park at the top of the hill. It's great for the sights." Kyle thanked Lucy as he gave Dingo a tender shake and pointed to the door so she would know what he was up to.

Dingo followed Kyle down the stairs and then up the sidewalk to the top of the hill in the dark. It took about twenty minutes to walk to the top of the hill. When the path narrowed, Kyle paused to gaze toward the northeast and look out at the signature San Francisco topography. He followed a street with his eyes that seemed to rise and fall, like a wave, on its way through town. The street lights glowed through the palm trees, and everything looked grainy, masked in this evening fog. He turned all the way around to gaze in every direction. He grasped why people adored this city as he could feel himself becoming emotional at this scene. From the hill, he could see the office buildings in the city's center, and to his right, Kyle saw the glow from the lights of another bridge going across the bay to the east. Far to the south, he could see lights from the next city and the faint silhouette of mountains in between. Spinning all the way around, Kyle could barely see the mountain's curve in the dark, far to the north that he crossed with Lucy and Dingo yesterday. This mountain seemed to rise up out of the dark and fog, and then it looked to him like it was floating on the fog. He stood still for a bit to gaze at it, but then it just returned to being an ordinary mountain.

He knew San Francisco was unique for other reasons, but this scene was overwhelming too. Kyle slowly pivoted one last time to take in all the sights and then led Dingo back down the hill.

Kyle followed Dingo up the stairs and then opened the door for her. Stella was still at the table and turned to ask over her shoulder, "How was the hill tonight?"

"The view was overwhelming. All the lights through the fog added an unearthliness."

Stella nodded her head. "Yes. For me, it's like looking through a magical kaleidoscope sometimes."

Lucy leaned to look out the kitchen. "Maybe you'd want to take her to the beach on the other side of town. How do you think she'd do on a bus? Public transportation will take you anywhere you want to go in the city, and they're great with dogs."

"That sounds like a great idea. I know she'd do fantastic." Kyle pointed at the stairs. "I'm gonna do a little reading before bed, so I'll see you in the morning."

In unison, Stella and Lucy said, "Goodnight. We'll see you guys tomorrow."

Dingo followed Kyle as he explored the neighborhood around Lucy and Stella's house for a few hours the next afternoon, and the next day the pair caught a bus out to the edge of town. The bus stop was right at the beach. They got off the bus and crossed one street to get to the water. Because it was the middle of the week, the beach was almost empty. They walked to the water so Dingo could play in the surf. Looking at his shoes and glancing up at the waves, Kyle made his way across the sandy beach. He decided this clip-clop sound of his footfall was more of a swish-swash sound now, like when a smaller wave meets the sand of the beach. Kyle stared out over the water, watching a sailboat that didn't seem to move much across the horizon. Kyle thought back on all his aviation weather. *There's lots of wind on the beach here, but maybe there's very little out there by the boat.*

Kyle had seen pictures of the S.F. piers and thought that would be an excellent place to take Dingo, and after a while on the beach, Kyle turned to walk back across the wide beach to the boardwalk. He looked back at Dingo when he was halfway across to notice she'd stopped to stare at a man fishing from the beach. *I saw Dingo noticed the Kite surfers in the waves too. It must be a strange sight for her 'cause even I think these are quirky pastimes.*

Dingo finally caught up with Kyle when he was almost to the boardwalk that paralleled the beach. Kyle had noticed a café about two blocks down with a long wooden bench facing the beach. He could enjoy a cup of coffee while resting in the sun, as the next bus wouldn't be at the stop for another 45 minutes.

After enjoying his coffee near the beach, they wandered to the bus stop. The bus dropped them off near the piers. As Kyle walked along the walk, he again noticed the subtle swish-swash sound his footfall made. While gazing out at the island prison, he tried to decide if that swish-swash sound would change back into a clip-clop sound when he walked on cement again. Kyle heard a commotion above him, and it surprised him to see an explosion of colorful little birds in the branches above his head. He had heard about these vibrant little birds from Lucy, and here they were in the branches of a tree. Kyle hadn't expected to see this wondrous sight as it seemed a bit far-fetched for parrots to be living in this cold city, yet they looked very healthy and happy up there. It sounded to Kyle like they were screaming at the top of their little lungs, but they were probably simply casually chatting about something they could see from up there. It seemed to him like an exceptional treat to witness this explosion of color and sound.

San Francisco is quite overwhelming: Full of sights and sounds that are maybe overwhelming for the senses. Like visually overwhelming when I saw the city at night from the hilltop, or overwhelming for the ears, like that flock of little birds. However, all these things seem to be just simple amusements that don't inspire wisdom like John was talking about.

The next morning before breakfast, Kyle was consumed with thoughts of wisdom and decided a walk on the beach with Dingo might help. Sensing the silence in the house, Lucy and Stella determined a walk on the beach would benefit them, so they walked down the stairs of their home, into the early morning fog, and down to the beach across the street. Peering through the mist, Stella could discern a person walking with a dog. Lucy and Stella decided it was probably Kyle and Dingo, so Stella called up the beach to them, and Kyle and Dingo turned to wait.

When Lucy and Stella got near, Kyle said, "I'm glad I ran into you two 'cause I was just pondering wisdom, and maybe you can help me with that. What do you think makes a wise master?"

Stella said, "Well, there was this person I worked with on a house years ago. Everything he constructed had a magical quality to it. How he put things together to make that structure hum was really cool because he'd never done construction before. No one would have called him a master builder, but I think he definitely built things with wisdom and a master's touch. I guess wisdom can show up anywhere and in many forms."

Lucy looked off into the fog resting on the ocean as if seeing something in that dense grey. She slowed her pace slightly, and everyone else turned to look searchingly into the mist except Dingo, who stared at Lucy. Lucy resumed her stride and looked up the beach, speaking softly. "I went to study with a great master in India. There, a wise master is called a guru. Although this guru was already an enlightened being, his stated mission was to assist all other beings to attain the same wisdom. He did that not by performing wisdom but by pointing out wisdom in his disciples. Telling another of wisdom within and that person having an actual experience of their own wisdom are two different things. There's a difference between the one that does something wise and the one that only says something wise. When we speak, it's mostly from thought, but we can choose to act through wisdom. I spent years in the guru's presence, always showing me the wise things I did, and eventually, I could almost see the wisdom within."

They walked up the beach in silence. Stella broke the silence and talked about the wisdom she was discovering within. "There's an improvisational acting class I'm taking. The instructor shares some guide-line for us to consider while we perform and tells us to allow ourselves to uncover what he calls, 'First Thought.' It seems to me that 'First Thought' would be the same as grace or wisdom. It's interesting that some really struggle with even finding it, let alone allowing that out."

Kyle turned to page four in his newest book a few days later while Dingo played in the sand by the ocean when Lucy came down to the beach to chat. "I had a student today in one of my classes that had a similar issue to yours regarding fear. I thought maybe you'd benefit from the ideas we discussed, so I wanted to share them. This woman talked about how she noticed her breath sometimes stopping from fear. I told her that fear is simply an idea that can cause a physiological reaction. I also told her that having a rational understanding is seldom helpful when dealing with an emotional situation. The woman said, 'Yeah, that's true. A rational understanding probably won't help.' But then she started talking about her visit to a park east of here. There was a herd of deer that would visit her tent every morning. You can imagine a deer being very watchful, and as she stood and watched, she saw the breath didn't ever stop. She watched the steam from a deer's breath through the morning fog and said she was in awe. She asked, 'Why is it so hard for me to do that?' I told her that a deer is constantly alert. Still, it doesn't seem like it will wear itself out by halting the breath and unnecessarily worrying about what might happen. However, we humans might have an adrenaline rush, and our breathing gets all weird, and the situation doesn't even call for a fistfight or running away. So, we're left with fear always being present in us or trusting our grace will always be available. I told that student I don't want to spend my life anticipating the worst-case scenario, so I'll live with the trust."

Contemplating the ocean for a bit, she resumed the story she shared with that woman. "A deer is a graceful animal because of its connection to its breath. Maybe the deer will pause the cycle temporarily, but because the breath is so much a part of their being, any time spent away from breathing just seems to strengthen that connection."

Kyle looked at Dingo and pondered Lucy's wisdom. He wondered if this animal was connected to its breath, like the deer in her story. He slowly lifted his gaze from Dingo to look out over the water and noticed a few pelicans flying north. Kyle's eyes returned to their spot on the beach, his toes peeking through the sand. He slowly lifted his gaze to Lucy and asked, "I had heard that all that stuff might have something to do with the fear of death."

Lucy nodded, saying, "Maybe it does, but we never know when that will be, so our best bet is just to do our grace in this moment."

Kyle bobbed his head, saying, "I'm going to try doing just that."

Lucy made a perfect impression of a famous movie character while pointing at Kyle, smiling, and with a bit of consternation in her voice, said, "No! Try not! Do or do not! There is no try."

And then, motioning towards her home, she said in her normal voice, "Let's go have some dinner. Stella's waiting for us."

Kyle smiled at the impression, "Nice." He nodded and followed her.

Each day at Lucy and Stella's would start at five am with yogic breathing and postures. An impressive breakfast of fruits would follow. Shortly after Lucy went to her studio, Kyle would stroll down to the beach with Dingo, taking off his shoe so he could walk barefoot. As he walked along, the sand would squeeze between his toes, and he'd feel his shirt billowing in the wind, then focus on his breath for a bit. He would walk along the beach to find a good spot to continue reading and spend most of the day reading his book, playing in the sand, and staring at the waves with Dingo.

One evening Lucy was teaching a late workshop at her studio, and Kyle discussed possible meanings behind his journey over the evening meal with Stella. She asked, "What do you think the purpose of your travel might be?"

Making a question mark with his face, Kyle said, "I've got no clue what I'm doing out here." After a long, thoughtful pause, he continued, "I've never really discovered my purpose back home, though one probably doesn't have anything to do with the other."

After pondering his statement, Stella said, "Maybe one doesn't have anything to with the other, or they could be the same thing. Either way, not having an answer is a great place to start, and you never know; something you think of as a tiny thing may have a huge impact on you." She stated firmly, "Putting some distance between you and what you thought was your life was probably hard, but a powerful first step. Do you remember when Lucy was talking about grace the other day? If you focus on leading with your grace, the other stuff just seems to fall into place." She added with a smile, "But this could be just the perfect vacation for you and

Dingo." Stella casually motioned toward Kyle with her fork, "In any case, just relax because you can't share grace when you're uptight."

Pointing to the carrots, Stella said, "Those are the last for this season from our garden. Have some more if you like." Kyle glanced over at Dingo as he reached for the serving dish with the carrots saying, "Thank you, I will have some more."

As Kyle snuggled into his sleeping bag that night, he saw his journal on the floor next to him, so he grabbed his pen to jot down some thoughts.

Lucy and Stella talk about grace a lot, but I haven't figured out what they mean, so I wonder about it often. It seems like grace sometimes means flowing in a situation like seaweed, and other times, it means standing firm like an unmovable rock. Grace and breathing seem to be connected, but I can't see how. Dingo appears to be graceful. She knows when to go with the flow and when to stand firm, but I don't seem even to grasp that concept. How can someone that drinks out of the toilet get it before me? Maybe I flow when I should stand firm and stand firm when it'd be better to flow. That's another contradiction that makes no sense to me, and it seems that Lucy was talking about something interfering with or covering up grace. Maybe the truth is somewhere in the contradiction.

I wonder if breathing is somehow connected to the attainment of wisdom. I think I'm going to hunt mellow breathing from now on. I look at Dingo and see that she's always breathing.

As he thought more about grace, a haiku started forming.

be graceful like grass

and unmovable like rock

see grace in all things

Kyle put his journal back on the floor next to him and snuggled deeper into his bag to finish the last few pages of his book. After completing the novel about the trials of a female hiker, it occurred to him, *She didn't have a dog with her, and a dog was maybe just what she needed so that her journey wasn't so rough. She emphasized all the troubles she was having on her way as if to say,* "See what could happen on a trip if you're not prepared?" Kyle believed not being prepared had been remarkably advantageous on his journey, and with a knowing smile, he thought *Ignorance is bliss. Being over-prepared could make a journey go in a particular direction, which might be the opposite direction of where you should go. Everything seems to be going just fine with my journey. So maybe this author is just overthinking her journey and offering a gloomy outlook.* Just as he said that to himself, an image of a spaceship appeared in Kyle's mind making monotonous loops around the planet called "truth."

Through Lucy's instruction, Kyle discovered that as soon as he focused on the air entering his body, he would become very interested in what was happening on this planet. As he shifted to sit up in his sleeping bag to perform his new breathing exercise, Kyle noticed Dingo stirring from her slumber to look up at him. As he started the first breathing cycle, Dingo laid her head back down.

The next day, Kyle found himself on the beach again. Occasionally Kyle would glance over the top of the book he was reading to look at Dingo playing near the surf. The sun was almost blinding as it sparkled off the smaller waves out beyond Dingo. She would furiously dig a hole in the sand that filled with surf every few seconds, and when the wave was gone, so was most of the hole. Undaunted, she'd start the whole process again. Kyle chuckled at her endless drive in this repetitive endeavor. Out of the blue, she stopped mid-dig and stared out across the water. Kyle watched her then walk up to where he was sitting in the sand and stand over him, patiently watching. Something just happened, but Kyle didn't know what it was. With a shrug, he got up, collected his book, brushed the sand from his clothes, and turned to walk toward Lucy and Stella's house. Dingo followed him up to the house and then led him up the stairs. Kyle opened the door for Dingo.

32

"Hey! Hello Dingo." As she walked by, Lucy leaned over to glide a hand over her wet back.

Stella pointed to the oven, "My bread will be done soon, then we'll eat. How was the beach?"

"The beach was awesome, as always. Dingo scratched this shell out of the sand." Kyle held up the shell and then placed it gently in Stella's hand. "It's a gift from us, and I think it's time for us to hit the road too."

Stella made an aww sound, and one hand found Dingo. "Thanks, girl!" Looking at Kyle, "You know we'd love for you guys to stay."

Kyle said, "It's been a great rest from traveling, and I've learned a lot, but I feel there's another place for me to be." Kyle let his gaze come to rest on the girls, saying, "That probably doesn't make a whole lot of sense, does it?"

Lucy and Stella both nodded and affirmed with a smile, "No, we get it!"

Kyle turned towards Lucy. "Thanks for showing me that breathing exercise. I use it a few times every day. It seems like for a few minutes after the exercise, I can't even remember what was so important I'd given up breathing for. Whenever I look at Dingo, she's always taking a full breath. The cycle never stops with her."

"That's awesome! I'm glad it's so helpful, and I'm guessing that you won't ever stop breathing after a while of practicing pranayama. Dingo is a great one to mimic. Animals are often the source of inspiration for humans. The physical postures in Yoga are named after the animals that inspired them." Pointing at Dingo, "You've seen her go into a play bow with her front paws way out in front? All Yoga students know what pose the teacher means when the teacher says, *go into downward-facing dog*. It'll look like a room full of dogs in a play bow." Glancing at Stella, "The trick is not to just mimic these things but to find the real-world benefit of these things we see." Pointing at Kyle for emphasis, she said, "My friend, you are on that path to discover." Lucy leaned over to pet Dingo, "I'm sorry to see you both go, but I'm sure you'll have a joyful journey."

33

Stella said, "I was getting used to having you guys around, and I'm sad to see you travel on, but when you get a hit to do something, it's not like you can set it aside for a better time." "I can give you guys a lift partway, although I have a friend heading down to L.A. in a couple of days." Turning to Lucy, "Isn't Helen planning a trip down there?"

Lucy declared, "She is. I'll give her a call." Turning to Kyle, "Maybe you can catch a ride with her."

4 Creating from emptiness

On the morning of their travel to L.A., Dingo watched from the stairs as Kyle put his pack in the trunk of Helen's car while Helen hugged Lucy and Stella. The sun was just rising, and the highway was only about 20 minutes from the house, so they'd be headed to L.A. soon. When Helen stepped back, Kyle looked toward Lucy and Stella, saying, "Thanks for the visit; I'm glad we got to stay. I learned a lot."

"We learned a bunch while you were here. It was thought-provoking talking about wisdom."

Stella buried her nose in Dingo's fur and murmured something, and Dingo turned to give her one gentle lick on the cheek, then descended the rest of the stairs in front of Helen's car.

Helen and Kyle were soon on the highway heading south. The two conversed a little about the direction and the endpoint, but Helen said, "I've made this same trip so many times that any new course-plotting might be debatable. I've even got the drive whittled down to under 7 hours."

As they chatted on the drive, Kyle learned the people Helen was meeting in L.A. had formed a musical group when they were in San Francisco. Helen told Kyle, "And when the group moved to L.A., I stayed behind to be near my other family. They are good people, and I like being around them, but I love visiting my friends in L.A. too. I play the keyboard but also sing in the group, and sometimes we switch it up, and I play other instruments. She added a somewhat philosophical statement, "I don't think you can challenge yourself artistically, or in life, without people around.

Kyle asked, "What do you mean about challenging yourself?"

Helen said, "I guess I mean, it's impossible to ask yourself a question to which your mind has already formed an answer. Most of the questions people ask themselves already have some sort of answer, so those questions are a waste of time and aren't truly challenging. I think it's better to have others around that might challenge you. You probably won't know what they will ask, so you're more likely to seek an authentic answer." Turning briefly to Kyle, "It's kinda like the first time I was asked to play a different instrument than the one I usually play in the band. I was sure the answer was 'NO, I can't play another instrument,' but a person challenged me to examine my feelings from many different angles, and I discovered an answer. People sometimes think that playing a musical instrument would be very different than 'real life,' but feel like how you do any one thing is how you do everything. Discovering the similarity in how you approach a task could show many missing pieces of the puzzle simultaneously." Helen shrugged, saying, "But that's just my story, and the path is maybe different for everyone."

Kyle wanted to understand this idea of challenging because he felt like the core of his journey was a challenge and said to Helen, "I feel like my journey is a colossal unanswered question. I have no idea what that question might be, but I feel like I've challenged myself to seek an authentic answer."

Helen raised her eyebrows as she said in surprise, "You are *absolutely* challenging yourself. However, there are two parts to that equation of challenging. I think of it like a *question and answer*, kind of like a *call and response*. A wolf howling would be the call, and listening intently would be where the response comes in. So you challenge yourself to find and ask a question, then challenge yourself to be still so you can listen intently." Helen glanced at Dingo and continued her thought, saying, "Maybe the challenge wouldn't have to start outside you at all 'cause it all originates in your heart anyway, though most people can't hear their hearts over the commotion in their lives, and most just stop even trying to listen.

Kyle said, "Kinda like San Francisco?"

Helen turned to Kyle. "Yeah! Sort of like that. San Francisco can be really noisy, and it's sometimes hard to pay attention with all those things that might catch your attention." Helen paused to consider that idea and then continued, "The ultimate challenge might be to witness your own emptiness and then create from that emptiness. The creation that is entirely distinctive to the individual is usually too taxing for people, so they try to fill the emptiness with money, people, or places; anything to keep from seeing and feeling the emptiness. I see that a lot in the city."

Kyle stared out the window as he pondered, challenging himself and about creating from emptiness. "How would emptiness and creation be tied together?"

Helen said, "Emptiness is the start of all creation. Nothing is created from thin air or by duplicating someone else's creation. Creating that way would be like painting with the same form as Picasso and declaring it all yours or maybe kinda like doing a cover song. It might be an awesome song, but it's still just your impression of it. I think true art starts from scratch or emptiness."

"I think I kinda understand what you're saying." Kyle returned to gazing out the window while Helen talked about something she called 'the dark night of the soul.' He thought *Helen seemed to have wild philosophical ideas, and it's challenging to follow her line of thought. Still, it's just really wonderful to be around someone who enjoys thinking and sharing about their journey. That is probably just what obscure philosophical thought sounds like.* Kyle continued nodding as they rode along but could vividly picture his spaceship silently gliding toward him through the darkness of space.

The conversation turned to books as they both liked to read. Helen chatted about a book Kyle had not read, saying, "There's an excellent book I've read over and over. The image on the cover is some castle or church shrouded in mist, and there's a critical message in the pages that you should probably seek out." She glanced in the back of her car, looking over a pile of books. She pointed to it, "There it is, next to Dingo's paw. You can take that one 'cause I've read it like ten times." Kyle reached in the back to retrieve it and thought with a smile, *Now I've got two books. Maybe I should always carry a backup book.* Kyle started to read his new book right away.

A few hours later, Helen parked her car in a driveway and, with a sigh, said, "We're here!" Kyle placed a bookmark in the pages where he was reading and looked out the windshield. Someone from the house was coming to meet them. This stranger hugged Helen intensely, saying, "I hope you're going to stay awhile this time."

The stranger put a hand out to Kyle, saying, "I'm Miguel." Helen replied with an introduction, "This is Kyle, and that's Dingo in the back." Miguel nodded, shaking Kyle's hand, saying, "Helen told me about your journey. I was thinking about it, and maybe tomorrow, if you'd be ok with us taking you a bit farther, there's a national park to the east. It's not really south, but it's an excellent park you might like to visit. "

Kyle said, "That might be cool. Thanks, Miguel. I'll think about that." Turning to Dingo, Kyle asked, "Is there a park around here for Dingo to run around?"

Miguel pointed, "Yeah. Just two blocks up this street and then right on Elm. You can't miss it about a half a block down."

Helen told Kyle, "I'll be cooking dinner in about half an hour or so."

"That's cool; we'll probably only be an hour or so."

Kyle opened the back door, and Dingo burst out. He smiled, "Not much for cars. Huh?" As Kyle followed Miguel's directions to the park, he realized how much he'd missed walking too. They reached the park, and Kyle opened the gate so Dingo could join the other dogs in the park. While the dogs played, Kyle sat on a bench nearby and pondered, heading east.

Nothing came to him, and he could faintly see his spaceship as if distantly approaching, so he focused on his breathing.

Kyle pondered if traveling east was a good idea and decided it <u>was</u> a good direction after a while. Kyle was anxious to tell Miguel and presumed Dingo had lost interest in the other dogs, so the pair wandered back to Miguel's. Kyle came in through the kitchen door and said, "You know Miguel, I'd like to start heading east, and that'd be great if you guys took me part of the way."

Miguel turned to the pair, saying, "Awesome!" and looking at Helen with a questioning look, "We'll go about ten?"

Helen nodded to Miguel offering Kyle a plate at the same time, saying, "Dinner's ready."

Later that night, he spread his sleeping bag on the couch and opened his journal to a blank page.

One of the books I've read talks plainly about wisdom, saying that the individual probably won't know wisdom without it being developed through some experience. Maybe, my problem is that I need more experiences to gain wisdom. That book made it seem like wisdom is some kind of secret only meant for a select few, though I watch effortless displays of wisdom and grace from Dingo. Maybe somehow, she's one of the select few.

Through the challenge I've given myself, maybe I'll discover emptiness. Kyle shook his head and wrote, **Could wisdom and grace really be found in emptiness that Helen talked about? I'm doubtful.**

Dingo makes me wonder about dogs' wisdom that they only share through silence. Some have said that dogs don't have the capacity to think, which is their downfall, but I wonder if people are trying to catch up to them somehow. Kinda like dogs might know something humans don't. Dingo probably already knows emptiness. Perhaps dogs just cut out all that excess complexity of thought and grow their wisdom. I remember someone alluding to the fact that wisdom could be stolen by

thinking, and it seems like I'm trying to hunt wisdom and grace like a wild animal with all my complicated thinking.

emptiness into

wisdom that evolves into

grace which is hunted

I must be over-using my capacity to think, and possibly that is the same as pushing wisdom away instead of causing it to draw near. I wonder if creating some silence would allow wisdom nearer, and maybe that's grace.

I wonder if some sequence of events must occur to attain wisdom: Like knowledge, silence, and finally, wisdom. I wish I had thought to ask John about the sequence because I can only rely on Dingo to do silence. Maybe the answers I seek are hidden in complexity. I can't think the answers would be in something as uncomplicated as simplicity or emptiness. Maybe Dingo has some advantage in that way.

The other morning on the trail, Dingo gazed at me with an unusual expression. She often looks at me with a smile in her eyes and a wag in her tail, but this was something different, and I got the impression there was a question in her gaze. She seemed to be asking me, "What's next?" I felt like telling her I had no idea what was next. Maybe it looks to her like I know where I'm going or what I'm doing, but most days, I'm so scared I feel like crying. Maybe not knowing what's next and simply doing everything with grace, like Dingo, could be the wisest action. As John said, 'Taking a step back' might be the only cure for my massive anxiety and confusion. Still, I wonder if taking a step back is easier than it sounds because taking that first step was very difficult. I can't imagine how hard the next one might be.

Kyle looked over at Dingo resting on the couch and wrote.

If only I could be as graceful as Dingo.

5 Love is thicker than water

After a few days of camping, where Helen and her friend dropped them off, Dingo and Kyle made their way east along the side of the road from the park. The pavement next to them was just starting to radiate heat. Kyle glanced down in the dust, noticed footprints from someone ahead of him, and looked up to see someone resting in the shade about a quarter mile up the road.

As they got closer, he could see it was a man about his age, and he kept glancing at the hand that was on the other side from Kyle. Kyle thought maybe he hurt it. Kyle walked under the sign, thankful to be in the shade, and took off his pack to sit down, saying, "Hey, I'm Kyle, and that's Dingo." Dingo circled behind to rest, which seemed odd to Kyle because she always sat right in front, almost on his foot. The person said nothing as he got up to stand in front of Kyle. He held out the injured hand, and Kyle noticed something shiny in it. Just then, Kyle felt a rumbling in the ground and turned to look for the freight train behind him, but he only saw Dingo creeping forward with hackles up. She was producing such an ominous growl that he felt more than heard it. Her teeth were bared in such a terrifying way that Kyle's eyes went wide, and he flinched. The person finally spoke, saying, "Shut that dog up and give me what you've got." Kyle turned to the man, about to explain that he had no idea how to turn this werewolf back into that fluffy puppy but stopped short, seeing that the shiny thing in his hand was a knife. He gasped at the sight, and then things seemed to go into hyper-fast forward. Dingo was suddenly latched onto that guy's arm. There was a shriek and then a puff of dust on the ground where the knife was dropped. That puff of dust held Kyle's attention, and when he finally looked up, that guy was sprinting away about fifty yards down the road with Dingo close behind. They disappeared over the rise in the direction they'd just come from.

Kyle waited for Dingo in the shade of that sign for what seemed like an hour. He looked down the hot, empty highway, worried that maybe that person had turned on Dingo and somehow injured her. A few minutes later, he noticed a car coming over the rise. As it got closer, he could see it was a highway patrol car, and Kyle got up to flag him down, but the cruiser pulled onto the shoulder and stopped. Kyle looked through the windshield and could see Dingo in the back seat. He pointed at her with a question on his face. The officer said through his window, "So, she's with you?"

"Yeah, that's Dingo. She's traveling with me. Where did you find her?"

The officer stepped out of his cruiser, saying, "I found her walking this way up the road a few miles. I just left the hospital in the town a few miles further west, where I took a complaint from a gentleman about a vicious dog by this road who attacked him for no reason."

Kyle raised his eyebrows and slowly produced the knife he picked out of the sand to hand it over to the officer, saying, "Well, you can return this to him then. He dropped it when Dingo chomped his arm."

The officer raised his eyebrows as he grasped the handle. "Was he just showing this to you?"

Kyle smirked. "In a way, but he only showed me the pointy end while demanding I give him my stuff."

The officer's voice changed as he held up the knife, saying, "So, he threatened you with this?" Kyle laughed, saying, "He certainly tried, but I feel kinda sorry for him."

The officer furrowed his brow. "Why's that?"

Kyle said, "He almost didn't have a chance to get the threat out. Dingo was on him in like half a heartbeat! That guy should probably find a new line of work that doesn't involve dogs or knives."

The officer chuckled, "I'm sure your dog gave him the message, loud and painfully clear." He turned toward the back of his cruiser, saying, "Maybe he'll re-think the options." while opening the door for the waiting Dingo to rejoin Kyle. Kyle crouched to be on a level with Dingo and spread his hands wide so she could get close, and he said adoringly, "Thanks for watching out for me, girl." He brought his arms around her to give her a snuggle saying, "That growl of yours is terrifying, and I'm glad it wasn't for me!"

Kyle turned back to the officer. "Thanks for bringing her back to me!"

The officer nodded in response and said, "My report is just going to say I found a knife on the side of the road where the bite probably took place. It is completely understandable to me that your dog would protect you. She acted in your defense, and I don't need to tell dispatch I found your dog or talked to you." The officer pointed to Dingo and said, "She would have made a great police dog." Winking at Dingo, he hooked a thumb toward Kyle and said to Dingo, "Take care of him." He waved to the pair as he got back in his cruiser. He made a U-turn, and Dingo stood next to Kyle as they watched the car disappear over the rise.

Kyle rested in the shade for quite a while, absent-mindedly petting Dingo. Turning to Dingo, finally, he said, "You know, girl, maybe there's more to you than just the dog I see."

Kyle rose and started heading east again with Dingo. As they walked along the side of the highway, Kyle counted in his head and figured this would be the solstice. The winter solstice marks the longest night of the year, and after, the days become longer. He turned to tell Dingo but stopped short as she'd probably be unimpressed with this astrological event.

Later that day, they walked into a campground by the road. It was sure to be a mild night as it would get very cold, but not a lot below freezing. The pair wandered around the campground and finally chose a site surrounded on three sides by trees to block the breeze that night. After he got the tent set up and was resting, he could hear campers making small talk a few spots away, and all of a sudden, he felt very lonely. That feeling grew when it got a little closer to dusk, and he heard the unmistakable sound of guitar and singing. *Was this the emptiness Helen was talking about?* Kyle wondered, *Maybe the emptiness I see outside is just a reminder of the emptiness inside, and there is no cure,* but just as Kyle was thinking of possible remedies for emptiness, Dingo got up and strolled over to the site with the sing-along. She sat down in the middle of their campsite and was immediately welcomed. Kyle followed Dingo's lead and, after a brief introduction, was soon enjoying the warmth of their fire and the people around it. A while later, Dingo got up and wandered back to their campsite, and Kyle followed, saying a warm goodnight over his shoulder.

Kyle noticed some clouds off to the east as he placed more firewood in his small fire ring. Kyle noticed a break in those clouds, revealing a planet. He turned back and saw glowing eyes watching him from under a nearby tree. Kyle recalled reading that dogs might be distantly related to wolves and maybe got domesticated by hanging around campfires on nights like this, accepting scraps, and collecting discarded food. As the fire dwindled, he would unroll his sleeping bag, and Kyle knew Dingo would come and lay very close in the tent. Maybe she did this to share the warmth. Maybe there was some more profound reason, but whatever Dingo's motive, it felt good to Kyle to have another being close while he slept.

campfire is warming

snapping and crackling flames

the dog moves away

As the evening got dark and the heat from the fire was almost gone, Kyle unzipped the tent door and crawled in with Dingo right behind. He snuggled into his sleeping bag and threw some of his extra clothes and sweater over Dingo. Kyle fell asleep thinking about the day's events and how Dingo saved him with her perceptiveness and care.

It felt to Kyle like two am when he woke again. He poked his head out, and it looked like it was about to rain a bit as he looked at the stars through the clouds. The thought of being looked upon by the universe suddenly occurred to him at that moment, and the universe might even consider his journey courageous. Kyle rummaged through his pack for the journal, knowing now that sleep would be elusive.

43

Though it took courage to leave, sometimes I question if there was any point in me leaving or being out here. I wonder if there's a particular direction I should be going in. I might be a thousand miles from where I started, but I feel no closer to any destination. I fear maybe Eddie and my other friends were right; I am just wandering around. I felt there could have, or should have been, some monumental meaning in my travels, but I've seen nothing. Maybe I missed the purpose of being out here and could just as easily have missed the meaning and stayed home. At least I'd be in my comfortable bed after spending the evening reading in my easy chair. My life may not have created some significant impact, but at least I was comfortable. When I was in San Francisco, I read a book at John's about wisdom and experience. I think it was written by someone who wasn't talking about creating discomfort to bring about wisdom. Still, there was something about 'discomfort as a path to wisdom.' Well, I can certainly say I'm very uncomfortable, but I don't feel any wiser.

I wonder if filling the emptiness with my thoughts makes me feel like the emptiness goes away. Helen was telling me something about the dark night of the soul, and as I look out the tent, it's incredibly dark out there—maybe that's what she was talking about. It seems like I'm surrounded by endless dark nights. Is the darkness a clue that I'm supposed to understand? Maybe darkness is comparable to the emptiness Helen was talking about. Perhaps I should have listened more to what she was saying. Am I supposed to discover something about emptiness? Will the experience of darkness or emptiness develop some innate wisdom in me? I just feel empty and scared, looking out at all the darkness. Maybe the questions about *experience* and *darkness* are only for philosophers to ask and understand. Perhaps I'll never understand, and those questions are like what my friend described as a 'unique thought' because I feel like all these unique thoughts only have loneliness and lack of truth in common. I wonder if there's some hidden truth I'm missing. I feel like I'm just going in circles. Why can't I be more at peace, like Dingo

safely in his tent

44

soothing sound of raindrops fall

next day the sun shines bright

After jotting the haiku down, he picked up the book Helen gave him but must have only read a few pages because he woke up in the morning with the book on his chest. The sun filled the tent, and Kyle was filled with his usual anxiety. This anxiety wasn't the crushing panic he felt before starting his journey, but it puzzled him that this anxiety would depart as soon as he began his morning activities. *I wonder if getting busy with something means shifting focus from an event I should be noticing, though I have many things that require my attention on the trail while hiking, like making my morning fire. Starting a fire, or really any activity, can be a potential distraction from seeing the emptiness that Helen talked about. I suppose the dark night of the soul Helen was talking about refers to something about the soul and not the darkness of the night because I feel the darkness most when the sun shines. Maybe the term is just a way to refer to a soul that is trying to ignore emptiness.*

Kyle was deliberating a possible connection between emptiness and his anxiety but suddenly halted, noticing the site with the singing campers was now empty. Kyle felt the vast loneliness inside himself again and wondered, *Is my anxiety somehow connected to my emptiness? Is the emptiness that I see _outside_ a reminder of the emptiness _inside_?* He thought back to his conversation with Helen for some word about emptiness he may have missed and realized he probably lacked some critical information. He thought, *Maybe noticing emptiness outside could be a trick I could use to see emptiness inside.*

Kyle watched Dingo as she made friends with the campers last night, and Kyle adored the sound of a guitar but thought he shouldn't fill the emptiness by playing an instrument or even forcibly filling it with a knife like that guy yesterday. *Maybe not filling the emptiness and simply looking at it was what Helen was talking about. Would a desperate act of violence with a weapon be kinda like playing a musical instrument to overlook emptiness? That would be like my building a fire or making a cup of coffee to avoid seeing emptiness.* Just then, Kyle's spaceship floated into view, and

45

he decided to walk. Kyle glanced at Dingo, and a haiku started to form in the silence.

emptiness; silence

one and the same in practice

the dog understands

Dingo trailed Kyle, and a few hours later, Kyle was, again, lost in thought about emptiness when a truck pulled over to offer them a ride. The woman that gave them a ride that morning only did so because she loves dogs, and Kyle just happened to be walking with one. If they had been riding in complete silence, that would have been fine with Kyle, but the lady kept asking questions about Dingo, "Do you think it's hard on her to travel? She asked other questions like, "How far has she walked?" and "How far are you going?" and "Does she seem worn out with all the walking?"

Kyle smiled when he told the woman, "No, but I'm kinda worn out."

Without acknowledging Kyle, she continued, "I'm going to visit my husband in Quartzsite. That's right over the border in Arizona. Do you have plans for this evening?"

"I'm just going to continue heading east, but thanks so much for giving us a lift."

She dropped them off a couple of hours later; he thanked her again for the ride, and just as they were about to get out, she said, "That seems to be a really well-behaved dog. How'd you train her?"

Kyle responded, "I didn't. I think she's just super smart." He paused to look up the road. Turning back to the woman, "I think what we believe dogs are capable of determines how much they can achieve." Waving goodbye to the woman, he turned to Dingo, and the pair continued walking along the highway. Kyle glanced back at Dingo marching behind him and felt envious of Dingo's gracefulness with which she seemed to move through life, but a subtle shift happened for him just then. He saw his spaceship coming into view and, without hesitation or debate, turned his attention to the clip-clop sound of his steps and his breathing. His breathing cycles thoroughly harmonized with his steps, and he could almost see his breathing cycle interconnected. Kyle thought back, and a feeling of excitement overcame him as he recognized this as the different breath John was talking about. This new breath seemed to have happened accidentally, but Kyle pondered his intention to move away from thoughts, and maybe that helped bring this synchronization into being. Kyle addressed the empty road and Dingo, saying, "But as soon as I started thinking about discovering my breath in the event, the calm feeling I experienced during the actual event was gone, and in its place were thoughts. It seems that spaceship shows up whenever my thoughts appear."

Since the ride from that woman to the border, the pair walked along the side of the road in silence. Kyle thought *it's nice just being in silence with Dingo. But I wonder how Dingo notices a change without a sound. Dingo seems to notice when I relax and smile. I used to think she's just a dog and couldn't possibly detect a difference in me, but her friendly tail wagging increased every time I looked over. Sometimes as she's passing by me, whenever I'm lost in thought, she'll softly poke at my leg with her nose and wait for me to look down at her. A friendly gaze is always waiting for me, and I always take a deeper breath when she does that. It's an excellent reminder to think less and breathe more.* Kyle glanced back at Dingo with a grin and nodded to himself.

Kyle got the feeling it was time to go north and kept glancing to his left, but there were no roads out there. He just saw an endless desert with old dirt paths and cattle trails leading farther into the sand and cactus. But a paved road appeared about 100 yards farther on that went northeast. Kyle chose the pavement and pointed out the road to Dingo as if she might be concerned about Kyle's inclination to go north.

As they started walking up that road, a pick-up truck with Nebraska plates pulled over, and the driver leaned over to call out the window, "Do you want a lift?" Kyle nodded yes and, pointing to Dingo, said, "We'd love one." The man from Nebraska stepped out and let down the tailgate, so Dingo could jump in, saying, "My wife is allergic to dogs." He gave Dingo a gentle rub on the neck and asked, "She won't jump out or anything, will she?" Kyle shook his head and said, "Nope," as he opened the passenger door to hop in. The truck pulled back onto the road, and the man turned to Kyle, saying, "My camper is parked in a town about 50 miles up the road. Every winter, my wife and I vacation in these parts to get away from that cold, white stuff, and we really enjoy coming down here to explore all the vistas. And even though it seems like you can see for a hundred miles down here, there are so many tiny features right in front of you."

Kyle nodded and, smiling, said, "Yeah, the winter is pretty mild here, and I love absorbing all those tiny facets of the desert." He paused and then turned to look at the driver. "And it sure is quiet out here."

The man agreed, saying, "Yeah, that's one of the other attractions for us. It's so silent down here that it almost seems to improve your hearing."

When they got to the center of town, the man pulled over, saying, "Well, this is it." He looked at Dingo out the back window and opened the door to head around the truck. The man let down the tailgate to his truck and pet Dingo asking Kyle, "Which way are you headed?"

Kyle shrugged and said, "I don't have a clue."

The guy pointed out some mountains to the northeast, "Well, that way's Prescott about a hundred miles."

Kyle said, "I think that's where we'll go then. Thanks so much for the ride!"

Kyle addressed Dingo as the truck pulled away. Turning, he asked, "Prescott is as good a destination as any, don't you think?" They continued on the side of the road, and after the better part of a day walking by the road, they'd been passed by an R.V. and four pick-up trucks. Kyle noticed the R.V. had a bumper sticker that read, "*Dog Is My Co-Pilot*." He knew the sticker was a play on the saying "GOD is my co-pilot," but he felt he owed Dingo a deeper understanding of their time together. He pondered the consequences of returning a condescending pat on the head or even a whimsical bumper sticker for some earth-shattering, essential information that this dog might have to share. *It's anybody's guess what influence this co-pilot might have on me.*

Climbing out of his philosophical musings, he noticed that way off to the north, some sheet-metal roofs were gleaming in the sun. He estimated those buildings to be a few miles off the road, but he knew that sometimes the desert plays tricks on your eyes and might be quite a bit farther away. As they walked north along the road, Dingo and Kyle would trade spots following each other, and Kyle felt somehow comforted by following Dingo up the road. *Maybe it's just the simple act of not having to lead all the time.* "Thanks for taking the lead, Dingo." She turned to look at him. Kyle thought this time, not so much from merely hearing her name. Smiling, he thought, *But the desert could be playing tricks on my mind, too.*

6 Evolution

As the two traded following each other up the highway, Kyle saw a dirt road that would undoubtedly lead to those abandoned buildings. Though the clouds didn't look like they held any moisture, he thought it'd be nice to spend a couple of nights under a roof and took a left turn over a cattle guard in the road to head in that direction.

Kyle could see recent tire tracks and some other animal prints in the dust of the road they followed, so they probably would not be alone. His footsteps made a new sound in the sand and dust of the desert. The clip-clop sound that had just before been significantly louder on the pavement changed when he reached the dust. This new dusty sound seemed to be like one continuous muted note. He put that together with Dingo's panting in his mind; collectively, those sounds had some meaning or pattern though Kyle couldn't put his finger on just what it was. It was the same frustrating feeling he had when he knew he'd forgotten something but couldn't remember what it was. Kyle knew thoughts were on the way to tell him the meaning of the sound, and he visualized his rocket ship silently gliding toward him out of the darkness. He focused on the air entering his lungs and immediately pictured the darkness engulfing the spaceship."

Some mountains loomed in the distance, and his walking slowed as he gazed at the range a few miles to the north. Maybe he'd find the answer in the silence of the mountains. Kyle thought, *Maybe the extreme silence of the hills could assist me in listening too. San Francisco was so loud, and subtle sounds easily get lost there.* But as Kyle stopped and gazed, he wondered, *Can the answer be found in silence because the message seemed to be cloaked in sound only a few moments ago?* He glanced down at Dingo, who was watching him knowingly. Kyle shrugged, smiling, *If the message is meant for me, I'll surely hear it, and the mountain range will be there tomorrow too.* He started walking again, and Dingo fell in beside him.

Kyle heard a vehicle approaching from behind when they were well out in the desert along the road. As Kyle turned to greet the vehicle, he noticed Dingo was nowhere to be seen. Kyle briefly wondered what she sensed. *Was it some sound? Maybe a smell? I wonder what it was.* An older guy stopped beside him in a pickup that used to be red. "Hey. I'm Jeb! You from around here?" Kyle said, "Nope." Pointing towards the deserted buildings, "I was thinkin' I'd camp out up there for a couple of days." Jeb, in turn, pointed to the empty seat next to him in the truck. "Well, jump in. I'll give you a ride." Jeb asked, motioning toward Dingo, who had silently reappeared next to his window, "Will she ride in the back?" Kyle nodded and thought the years of desert living must have made his vision so acute. Jeb quickly picked up that Dingo was a "she" without even looking at her, though Kyle had the idea that Jeb was probably watching Dingo hiding in the bushes this whole time. As Kyle stepped around the truck and lowered the tailgate to put his backpack in, Dingo simply jumped in. There seemed to be no need to motion her to the truck bed; she just knew to jump in. Kyle wondered, with a smile, *What else does she just know?* And climbed in next to Jeb. They bumped up the last mile or so of the sandy road, passing a sign that announced they had just arrived at THE BEST GOLD PANNING IN THE STATE.

Kyle learned that those abandoned buildings were actually an old mining ghost town museum, and Jeb was the caretaker. He gets one day a week to make the two-hour drive to town for any supplies he needs. When they came to a stop in the center of the ghost town, Jeb gave a quick tour by pointing through the dusty windshield. Aiming his finger at one shack, Jeb said, "You can use that old miners' cabin there while you're here, and since I don't get many visitors or much help way out here, I might ask you for a hand with some of the chores." Dingo took that as an excellent time to jump over the side and take many slurps from a half-filled pail of water by the well pump. Kyle leaped at the chance to help and said to Jeb, "Absolutely. I'd love to lend a hand. Just make a list."

Jeb stared at the ceiling of his truck. "Great, maybe a list is a good idea 'cause I can only think of one or two things now." Jeb moved the pick-up to a sort of sunshade. "Come on in the trailer while I put my groceries away." Kyle glanced over at Dingo, still at the well, as he stepped out of Jeb's truck and grabbed a few sacks of groceries before backing up to let Jeb grab some. He noticed a small pistol peeking out from under Jeb's jacket as Jeb reached to get another bag; Kyle shook his head at the sight of the pistol but then thought, *You probably have to be ready to defend yourself, way out here, against people like that guy the other day with the knife.* Kyle followed Jeb up the stairs and into the trailer. Since the trailer was under the sunshade, too, it was pretty chilly inside. Jeb asked a string of questions like where they were headed, where they'd been, their daily routine, and others. Kyle mentioned between answering the questions, "Dingo just found me a few weeks ago, so I'm not even sure she'll stick around." After talking briefly, Kyle turned to the door and said, "I'd better take my stuff up to that shack." When He opened the door to the trailer, Dingo was waiting for him at the bottom stair.

The pair walked through the silent town on the way to the miner's shack. Dingo leaped up the few stairs to the first building and followed Kyle along the boardwalk that connected the 10 or 12 buildings. She passed by Kyle as he stopped to gaze across the small dirt street at the enormous stamp mill. Thinking back on the conversation with Jeb, "There's a lot of very old mining equipment in this town. You'll see some of them all up and down the main street. The biggest is that 'ol stamp mill. The stamp mill is ancient and used to crush rock that might have contained gold. Some things haven't changed much over the years, and they still use something like that in mining today; of course, it don't look much like that one."

The enormous wooden timbers of the stamp mill were about 20 feet high and all sun-bleached from the Arizona sun. Kyle stared at the stamp mill, thinking *It just looks like a bunch of big hammers to me. It's just another way to bust open rocks, so it doesn't seem like there's been a lot of evolution over the years.* Pondering the relationship of evolution to emptiness, Kyle wondered, *Maybe evolution could happen in a totally different way.* Looking at Dingo for backup as if she'd approve or disapprove and seeing neither, he continued with his thought. *What if emptiness was the goal instead of the search for wealth?* Shaking his head at the doubtfulness of that thought and smirking at the image of miners searching for emptiness, he turned to continue up the boardwalk.

Jeb had said that back in the day, this was a busy little town that operated twenty-four hours a day. As Kyle walked through the town, he tried to imagine all the noise that would have surrounded him, but the only sound now was the soft clicking of Dingo's nails on the old sun-bleached boardwalk. Kyle followed her dusty paw prints on the walkway in front of the buildings. Peeking through the window at the dust-covered interior of one of the buildings, Kyle saw what appeared to be a dust-covered mannequin and felt an enormous emptiness that transcended simple loneliness. *These mannequins maybe show how the bartender pouring a drink or the sheriff locking a door would have looked. They might be saying,* "Look how cool things would be if nothing ever evolved." Kyle turned to follow Dingo towards their cabin with the sun going behind the mountains.

Kyle unrolled his sleeping bag on the miners' cot, feeling happy not to be sleeping on the ground. The concept of evolution would not leave him alone, and shrugging to himself, he thought, *Being out in the world could be a great place to practice seeing my response to things, but this ghost town might be the best place to see who Kyle truly is. Evolution might only occur if one knows who they are and then decide who they aspire to be.* Finally,

Kyle decided he didn't know how evolution might work and just prayed that he would find his path and not fritter away his life. Kyle thought, *Maybe if I could evolve but didn't, that could cause my massive anxiety.* Knowing that evolution is a concept that he might never grasp, he put it away for another time. He took one last look at the stars outside the window of the miner's cabin before slipping on the headlamp to find his journal.

I realized that jumping in to help Jeb could be just another distraction. I'm not debating about doing what I think is right or simply lending a hand to someone, but I fear getting lost in the safety of doing a task. I fear looking for some significance by being immersed in a task, like when I commanded immediate respect by fixing something or telling others about me being an aircraft mechanic. I'll miss that look of immediate respect, but I can see how those people weren't respecting wisdom because it doesn't take wisdom to be a mechanic. It is safe for me to perform some tasks from memory, but those probably wouldn't include any performance of wisdom. Getting lost in some task because I want that feeling of significance could indicate that I'm not on a path to discover wisdom.

Kyle nodded excitedly to himself and continued writing. **That could be part of evolution! I see so many people stuck in doing some task endlessly and never finding an authentic or unique expression that I wonder if those people might have missed evolving altogether. Some portray themselves as wise; seeking to sell what they say is a critical part of the path. It seems that evolution and wisdom can pass by both the one endlessly performing some thoughtless task and the one seeking to sell wisdom.**

I look at Dingo, and I can see no connection between the wisdom she shares and any possible reward that she might get. It's like the story of the Knight I saw in John's quest. Does wisdom emanate from emptiness? There seem to be so many pieces to this puzzle, and it's so frustrating to know I'm going in circles, asking kinda the same questions and getting the same answers. Is it possible that I have to slowly collect all the pieces to

the puzzle of wisdom, but Dingo's already evolved to integrate all the pieces of emptiness?

Kyle turned to see the book Helen had given him and decided it might be a relief to read more about the dreamer's adventures and focus less on his own inadequacies.

The next morning Kyle remembered his thoughts about emptiness and wisdom, opening and closing his eyes to experiment with distraction in the early morning light. Kyle found that even opening his eyes could be a slight distraction from emptiness. A little while later, he climbed out of bed and followed Dingo out the door into the first light. Kyle paused to look at the newly risen sun. Coyotes on a hill to the north yipped, coyotes to the east would bark in response, and then more coyotes to the west would chime in, creating a desert symphony.

Walking through town, Jeb waved from the window of the old saloon. The two stepped up on the boardwalk and through the door to find Jeb making his morning coffee in the back. He offered Kyle a cup, saying, "The first guests wouldn't be venturing out this far 'till ten or even noon. How'd ya sleep?" Kyle accepted the cup, saying, "Thanks. Even with Dingo sleeping on top of me, I slept soundly." Kyle pointed at the door with his coffee mug. "We heard a bunch of coyotes singing on our way over here. Do you think they'll come into town and attack Dingo?"

Jeb took a sip from his coffee, shaking his head. "They probably won't, but it's impossible to say what they're thinking." Nodding at Dingo, "She looks like she knows how to handle herself, and there's lots of smaller game for the coyotes to go after, so I wouldn't even consider it." Dingo went and sat on the boardwalk and soaked up the morning sun while the two remained near the coffee maker. She stared out at the now-silent desert, but Kyle couldn't help feeling that the desert wasn't silent at all as he looked through the window. Dingo seemed engrossed as if watching a favorite T.V. program, and again he felt envious of Dingo. *There's probably a great show going on out there if I could only hear it. Maybe what I think is absolute silence is just there to help me hear better. In truth, there probably is sound.*

Kyle shook his head at his line of thought, which even he couldn't follow sometimes. *Some invisible sound? How did I dream that one up?*

A couple of weeks later, following Dingo down the main street in town on their way to find Jeb, a warm breeze rose, gently touching Kyle on the back of his bare neck. He almost thought the breeze carried a sound and turned to see where it came from. Seeing nothing but the silent mountain range, he thought in surprise, *Did the mountain just speak?* Shaking his head at himself for having such an absurd thought. He turned to see Dingo watching him knowingly, and they continued their search.

The couple of days Kyle planned to stay there turned into about a month the pair spent helping with chores around the town. Jeb finally told Kyle, "There are a lot of two-man jobs I couldn't take care of before, so thanks for your help." Kyle was even helping with the visitors as he'd been schooled in the art of panning for gold by Jeb and was very comfortable teaching while Jeb visited with other guests or tended to chores around town. Kyle noticed Dingo enjoyed being around town, and it seemed like she had an immense soft spot for Jeb. One evening, out for a walk, Dingo stopped to stare off to a mesa in the east. The distant mesa looked to Kyle like it might be a hundred miles away. Dingo turned to fix her gaze on Kyle, and Kyle nodded while they continued their walk. The following day, Kyle told Jeb it was time for them to be getting back on the road. Jeb probably didn't want them to leave but told Kyle about a ranch up north looking for some assistance. He told Kyle, "You'd be perfect 'cause they only need help for a couple months."

A couple of days later, a family arrived about when Jeb had said people usually visit, and Kyle made small talk with Nancy and her family while he showed them how to pan for gold. He mentioned that he was going to help at another ranch up north in a couple of weeks, and Nancy offered the pair a ride as she was only a half-hour down the road and worked from home. "Just call when you're ready."

That night Kyle dug through the pack for his journal. He had some more thoughts about evolution and had to write them down.

Some say evolution happens in a particular way, like a staircase or going from point A to point B, but what if halfway up the stairs, you wanted a fantastic sense of smell and came back as a dog? What if you've had a thousand lifetimes and decided to possess a super complex language and come back as a dolphin? Why do we automatically assume someone to be at the bottom of the evolutionary staircase if they are a pig? Maybe evolution allows you to see how much you can achieve, whether you're a pig or a tree. I wonder if there is evolution in this life or if it just happens across lifetimes. What if the anxiety I feel is just part of me wanting to evolve more in this lifetime?

I remember a story about a young man going to see a very wise man in that book Helen gave me. The young man was told to wait a bit to see the wise man. The wise man told him to walk around and look at his beautiful palace while he was waiting. The wise man gave the young man a spoon to hold, and as he was going to look around the palace, a few drops of oil were placed in his spoon. As the young man moved around the palace and looked at the opulent rooms, the oil was forgotten and dropped from the spoon. The wise man noticed the oil was missing and mentioned to the boy that he probably got distracted, and the drops spilled out. It seems the story might have been about the boy learning how evolution could happen.

Maybe losing yourself in the experience of being, or doing anything in a lifetime, is like forgetting about the drops of oil in your spoon. It'd be great to have the extraordinary sense of smell of a dog or the astonishing intelligence of a pig, but forgetting it's just an experience would be like forgetting about the drops of oil in your spoon and might prevent you from evolving.

A few days later, Kyle borrowed Jeb's cell phone to call Nancy. He told her, "The other ranch would be looking for me to arrive in about a week and even has an old truck for him to use while I'm there. The ride to the other ranch would be a couple of hours, so I hope that's okay?" Nancy said, "That would be perfect because it's an excellent opportunity for me to get out of town." They decided on a time for the trip, a few days in the future.

The following day Kyle discussed his plans with Jeb, and Jeb took the news that they'd be leaving stoically. Kyle thought Jeb enjoyed having Dingo in town, and it seemed to Kyle that maybe Dingo was trying to get Jeb to re-engage with his surroundings through the visitors. Kyle could see Jeb had, perhaps, disengaged on purpose and possibly didn't wish to re-engage. Kyle thought again about his possible evolution and longing to be on his path. Jeb seemed to have a friendly, engaging personality that he'd share with the guests, but as soon as they'd gone, he'd revert to his "natural" persona. Kyle thought with a shrug; *Maybe he's just on that one step of evolution.*

On one of Kyle's last nights in the ghost town, he was inspired to compose another poem. The moon was so bright he could see all the contours of the surrounding hills and distinctly spot every pebble on the sandy path.

Seeing a half-moon

Wondering when it is full

Tonight lights up path

7 Follow the clues

Nancy drove into the parking area of the mining camp around nine am to pick up Kyle. He knew that Jeb would be alone again in this ghost town when they were gone, and he'd probably miss people being around. Kyle shook Jeb's' hand as he said, "Goodbye and thanks," and then climbed into Nancy's car. Jeb gave a solemn pet to Dingo, saying, "See you later, girl." Kyle thought it might be time for Jeb to live in a "real" town with people and dogs. Noticing Jeb's possible reluctance to engage or evolve, Kyle thought, *I wonder if my fear keeps me from evolving too.*

Kyle asked Nancy what she did for a living when they were out on the highway. Nancy said, "I work as a psychic and coach." She explained, "It seemed to me that people often have trouble moving forward with the wisdom they discover during our sessions, so I coach them along."

Kyle thought it seemed like he had trouble implementing any wisdom in his life and asked, "So Nancy, do you have any insight on my travels?

"Yeah!" She said, "You were correct in listening to that clue about quitting your job and just walking. In reality, your wisdom will shine through whether you are a musician or a mechanic, so it's sort of irrelevant what you choose to do for work. However, at times in our lives, it's necessary for us to kind of re-show ourselves that we have wisdom by being courageous enough to start something new. Any experience could have the effect of drawing out the wisdom we already have." Nancy paused for an inhale and a slow exhale before continuing. "Still, sometimes we must trust that the first scary step we take can lead to drawing out that wisdom. You've already taken that first step to hear the clues and draw out that wisdom; just be open to the next step.

Pausing, Nancy looked over her shoulder at Dingo. She said, "People may stare at dogs for years and then pronounce themselves experts on dogs. Glancing over at Kyle, "The next step might simply be allowing your thoughts to be a little more flexible."

Kyle scrunched his brow and turned to Nancy.

"What I'm saying is in relying on somebody else's formula, you won't allow your wisdom to come out. That formula might have to do with dogs or paintings, but it's only correct for the one that is projecting it. Granting permission for your thoughts to have the freedom to show up in a flexible way could be critical." Nancy pointed to Dingo. "In any case, watch her. She has many messages; you'll know how to interpret them when it comes." She saw the questioning look on Kyle's face and said with a knowing smile, "Just watch her; you'll be able to see."

Nancy continued, "There seems to be some all-powerful force in the universe called GOD, a higher power, infinite intelligence, or whatever that will always give you hunches and leave clues along your path. Whatever you call the source, please don't ignore the clues because they tend to get discreet and eventually disappear. No one else can tell you what the clue means because the clue only comes in a form you would understand. I've gotten huge benefits from the clues I received only because I was courageous enough to listen at all costs and not put my knowledge in the place of the response. Some of my knowledge may have made the clue easier to understand, but it also could have modified it. Thinking and knowledge seem to get in the way of hearing." She sensed Kyle getting confused and said, "Hearing the clue is not a skill that only the chosen few have, and you'll understand what I'm trying to say as you hear more clues." Pausing to glance at Dingo, Nancy continued, "Some are really good at getting quiet so they can hear the clues, and it's okay to mimic their behavior for a while."

Kyle didn't have much experience with psychics, and he was overwhelmed with all this new information and the idea that some power that he couldn't see or touch might help him along in his journey and leave clues just for him. It seemed too simple that success might be found in just hearing and following clues.

He also thought Nancy might have valuable insight into his crushing anxiety. He glanced at the sleeping form of Dingo as if she might provide some suggestion that he should reveal this information or withhold it. Taking her snoozing as an indication that she'd vote for full disclosure, he told Nancy about being consumed with anxiety. She looked over at him and exclaimed, "That's great!" Kyle wondered aloud about the sanity of psychics or if she even heard him. Nancy laughed at that and elaborated, saying, "It's probably just your heart beginning to speak again. Maybe your heart is screaming because you've ignored it for so long. Remember I was talking about clues, voices, and intuition? You're probably getting one of those, and until you become a listener and follower, your heart may scream to make itself heard." Turning to look at Kyle for emphasis, "When you hear a scream, be grateful for any sound you hear and treat it like a good friend waking up from a nightmare."

Kyle barely understood and visualized a swimmer struggling to lift themselves out of the water and onto a dock. He seemed to be that struggling swimmer and told Nancy so. Nancy responded, "There's a book you might like to read with some ideas we discussed. The cover has a blue feather on it.

Kyle wondered if the clues were like signs on the side of the road or if they were more subtle so that he might miss them. He composed a Haiku in his head as they rode along in silence, counting the number of syllables on his fingers.

questions might consume

always answers available

together make whole

Nancy interrupted Kyle's thoughts by telling him about the clothes and gear he'd need at the ranch. Kyle nodded and wanted to ask Nancy how she had become an expert on cowboy gear, but her advice sounded sincere and made perfect sense, so they stopped at a store where he could buy some jeans, work gloves, boots, and a hat. Kyle felt like an imposter looking in the mirror at this guy "decked out" in new cowboy clothes, but Nancy assured him he'd be thankful for the gear. With that, Kyle nodded to himself before going up to the check stand.

When they pulled into the ranch, Kyle was greeted by Kevin, the leading horse wrangler for the ranch. Kevin pointed to the bunkhouse for Kyle and said Dingo would get along great with the other five ranch dogs. Kyle turned to Nancy and said, "Farewell. Thanks for the lift. Nancy wished Kyle well. "It was a pleasure to give you and Dingo a ride. I think we had a great talk, too!" Nancy gave a pet and mumbled some words to Dingo before waving goodbye to Kyle and driving off.

As there wasn't much happening that day, Kevin accompanied Kyle and Dingo to the bunkhouse. While on the way, Kevin pointed to the truck Kyle would be using and casually mentioned a cave over his shoulder in the rocks above. He also gave a quick outline of where things were located on the ranch but said that he'd pick up stuff as he went along. Kevin pointed to his camper, saying, "Come on over; I'll be there about six tonight, and everyone meets in the office at 7 am."

After showing himself around the area, Kyle stopped by Kevin's camper later that evening. Kevin filled Kyle in on some general information about the ranch's history, and then Kyle and Dingo wandered back to the bunkhouse.

As Kyle settled in for the night, he turned to his journal. Nancy's words kept repeating to him about Dingo. She said, "Just watch her; you'll be able to see." Kyle thought, *This seemed to be a mysterious and somewhat crucial statement. I probably should have questioned her more about it, and I wonder if it had anything to do with allowing my thoughts to be a little more flexible.*

A funny thing happened with Dingo at the ghost town. A few nights ago, I found my sleeping spot on the floor of the miner's cabin and got into my bag. I started to read where I had left off in my book the day before when Dingo came to stand over me. She looked at me with an expression I'd not seen on her before, so I lowered the book to look back. She gazed at me intently for a few moments more, then lowered a bit so her throat gently rested on my throat. I immediately saw a cotton fiber slowly floating in a shaft of light and coming to rest on my throat gently. I laid still as I was frozen with confusion and a little apprehensive. After a few moments like that, she simply stood and walked back to her sleeping spot, and I remember thinking that was strange. I wondered if maybe she intended to walk past and tripped, so I soon went back to reading and was engrossed in my book. However, Dingo went through that very same routine on many of the following nights. After the third night, as she returned to her sleeping spot, I stubbornly searched for meaning. I found nothing concrete in the scientific explanations I came up with, and, in the end, I was left with a question and no answer. Sure, some dog behaviorists would say, "It's probably just her feeding time." Maybe they'd come up with some ideas, but I'm sure they'd be equally mundane and commonplace. But I think those explanations are an easy way to get

out of searching or asking more questions. I know there is a theory of some energy concentration in that area called the throat chakra. So maybe she was trying to fix my chakra, or perhaps she was trying to fix hers'? Was there maybe some message she felt compelled to get across, and gently resting her throat on mine was the nearest she could get to actually speaking?

All questions with no answers make me think there is no such thing as a concrete answer, though I feel the response could have been in one of the subtle clues I may have missed, like Nancy was talking about. She recommended allowing my thinking to be more flexible. I have no idea how I could do that, but maybe it has something to do with that quote I read. It said, "The only question worth asking is, "I DON'T KNOW." It seemed like some mumbo jumbo-double talk at the time, but maybe there's some wisdom there. Perhaps that is the essence of flexible thinking. Not rushing to some conclusion is a great way to keep gently looking for truth. Maybe the clue is so subtle that lighting on some conclusion would eliminate the possibility of seeing the clue. Does my orbiting rocket ship prevent the seeing of clues or truth? So many thoughts are rumbling around my head; if I keep paying attention to them, I may never see truth.

8 Follow your joy

Dingo trailed Kyle to the ranch office at 7 am for the very brief ranch briefing. There were five people in the office when Kyle walked in. Kevin gave a short introduction for Kyle, and this was followed by what seemed to be some secret language the ranch workers used to tell each other what needed to be done, by when and who would do it. Kyle couldn't follow any of it, and Kevin noticed the quizzical look on Kyle's face motioning for Kyle to join him after the meeting.

Kyle shadowed Kevin for the first couple of hours but then did some of the chores on his own. The chores on the ranch kept Kyle very busy, and Dingo would usually get tired of trailing Kyle around the ranch and find a shady spot to lie down and just watch him. Kyle occasionally took a break and sat in the shade with Dingo.

The next day, Kyle was pretty much on his own to do the chores. At sunrise, Kyle would be out feeding the 70 or so horses. After that, he and Dingo would ride over to the little "movie-set town" to empty trash, stock food and drinks for the visitors, and sweep out the buildings. By the time he was done with the town, the first guests would be arriving. Dingo would help him gather horses and then keep the guests entertained while Kyle helped brush and saddle. Because the horses had this done almost daily, they did everything very slowly and methodically. If the horse could complete the task with one move instead of three, the horse wouldn't even consider doing more than one. The horses would slowly stroll up to the rail for their morning brushing.

One morning, standing in the narrow space between two horses, Kyle paused his brushing of the horse to glance over his shoulder. Something moved and caught his attention, but seeing nothing except an empty parking lot behind, his gaze returned to rest on the spot of the horse right in front of his face where the sunlight fell. He immediately noticed his breathing matched the relaxed breathing of the enormous animal, and the shaft of light he was standing in contained a cloud of dancing dust from his brushing of the horse. Gazing at the dust floating in the shaft of light around the horses, the image of the cotton fiber resting on his throat immediately returned to him. Kyle looked over at Dingo, sitting on the porch, and wondered what the dancing fiber had in common with the dancing dust in front of me or that movement over my shoulder. Turning back to the horse, he continued with his brushing and saddling. *Maybe I missed seeing a clue in the parking lot.* He looked at Dingo again and thought, *If only I were as silent and relaxed as Dingo, I'd probably never miss a clue.*

By noon on the ranch, there might be some time for lunch, which was the only meal. The BBQ grill was going in that little town every afternoon, and all the ranch hands could get lunch there. Kyle could smell the BBQ grill smoke from the office when the breeze was slightly to the south. Kyle knew it was about lunchtime on the ranch, and Dingo would follow him to the truck so they could have lunch in the little town. Kyle had gotten used to Lucy & Stella's yogic diet, but the only veggies to be had on the ranch were the lettuce and tomato that came on the cheeseburgers.

The horses would have their evening meal as the last chore of the day, and everything would be wrapped up for the day by 7 pm.

That evening Kyle saw his journal lying near the door and realized he'd been creating a haiku in his head.

silence of the dog

imitate my co-pilot

wisdom will arrive

One afternoon the old ranch truck stopped running for him while he was doing his chores. Discouraged, Kyle walked back to the office, where they called Kevin off whatever he was doing to help. Kevin wandered over, leaned in the window, and started the truck right up. He then turned to Kyle with a smile and shrug. Kyle chuckled and shook his head as he and Dingo walked back to the running truck. Kyle wondered, *Does Kevin have a feel for how to make that truck work, or maybe this could be the lightness of cotton fiber that Dingo showed me, and perhaps the lightness of cotton fiber that he possesses influences other aspects of life? I can see an eagerness in all the animals to do something for Kevin and maybe try to guess what he might want. Is that just his knowledge of horses, or is he acting with grace and wisdom that might transcend simple knowledge? Maybe that lightness of cotton fiber is some vital link, but without simple knowledge, I don't think I could ever develop wisdom.*

The next day, Kevin had the hood up on the truck showing Kyle a little trick to get the truck started. Kyle pointed to a house on the hill. "Who owns that one?"

Kevin looked and said, "Oh, that one is on the ranch. The ranch owner and his wife live there. We don't see them much down here. It's somewhat irritating to me the way they handle that other ranch. The one you were at with Jeb. As long as it's making them some money, they don't even visit. Jeb's health has declined over the years, and he really needs help."

Kyle straightened up to look at the house as if seeing it for the first time. "A friend told me many people try to convert their wisdom into cash. I wonder if that's what he did?"

"You know, I never thought of it that way. The owner seems to have some wisdom, but maybe he did get off the path of pursuing wisdom somewhere so he could devote his time to making money. I guess it's a decision every person has to make, and he made his."

A few days later, Kyle passed by a group of people on his way to some chores in the ranch truck, and Dingo stared at the people from the passenger seat as they passed. Kyle suddenly felt like one of those old ladies that would always have to have their emotional support dog with them everywhere they'd go. He had become so used to seeing the omnipresent Dingo around that when she wasn't near, his growing concern caused him to re-examine the importance of Dingo. Maybe Dingo is like an emotional support dog, but her displays of grace and wisdom place her far above emotional support dogs. Kyle reached over to place a hand on her shoulder. Feeling the soft fur, he glanced over to see her return his gaze. Simply *with her presence, I think Dingo has made a massive impact on my journey. I get the feeling that Dingo isn't an emotional support dog because maybe she isn't supporting* what is *but guiding me to evolve into the wisdom I see. The path I would have taken without a dog wouldn't have brought me into contact with so many wise people.* A rock on the edge of the road jolted the truck, and Kyle's eye's snapped back forward so he could center the truck in the dirt tracks. When he stopped the truck, Kyle opened the door to step down on the street of the dusty town, leaving the door open so Dingo could find a spot in the shade.

Most every night, Dingo and Kyle were alone in the 8-bed bunkhouse on the ranch. It seldom got cold enough to light the little wood stove, which was good because as he looked out the door, all he saw was small brush among the rocks and that tree-like, giant 'Saguaro' cactus. The bunkhouse also faced that steep slope with the cave Kevin had mentioned. The dark entrance kept drawing his attention, and Kyle followed Dingo over to Kevin's camper that night. They found him much the same as every other evening. Kevin was sitting in a camp chair, beer in hand, gazing at the desert through his faded blue eyes. Pointing to the chair beside him, he said, "Welcome to my living room. I only get one channel, but it's fascinating! Look." Motioning with a sweeping arm, Kevin gestured to the entire desert around them. Smiling at that, Kyle sat in an extra camp chair. He pointed at the cave, "Tell me the story." Dingo jumped up on a flat rock near the camper, and Kevin got up to grab some beers from his camper.

Kevin paused with his hand on the door-nob, saying, "Nobody knows for sure about that cave, but one theory is that conquistadors used it for a hidey-hole. The conquistadors maybe came through this valley and stashed rifles they didn't want to carry in that cave or the spoils of some conquest to be reclaimed on their return journey. They could have forgotten, couldn't find it again, or they got way better loot and didn't even bother. In any case, it's hard to get to now." Kevin pointed to the rocks at the base of that steep slope, "There was a landslide, some years back, that started just under the cave entrance and took away all the solid footing. Now there's a rubble slide for the 200-foot drop to the wash below. At 64, there's no way I should be scrambling around those rocks." He looked at Kyle, saying, "Maybe someone younger could come at that entrance from above." Kyle felt like going up there right then, but Kevin said, "Wait until full daylight; That cave ain't going nowhere" Kyle promptly forgot about the conquistador gold as Kevin launched into a dissertation about antique firearms. Kyle hadn't thought the history of weapons would be so fascinating, but the chronicle of the firearm is incredibly far-reaching. While making his way back to the bunkhouse that evening, Kyle thought, *Kevin is very knowledgeable, which can be entertaining, but when he does something with wisdom and grace, it far surpasses his basic knowledge. I'm surprised because I didn't expect to find wisdom and grace way out here in the middle of the desert.*

The next day, as he stood beside a horse pen waiting for a water trough to fill, Kyle noticed he cast the shadow of a cowboy. Kyle remembered when he was working at an airport and was asked to bring a headset out to a waiting pilot in an aircraft. Kyle noticed the shadow of the headset in his hand and thought, *That's the shadow of a pilot that I'm casting. I wonder how many other forms my shadow could portray, like the animal lover, the yoga teacher, the surfer, the bicyclist, the coffee shop patron, or even the one searching for conquistador gold. Am I limited to one shadow, or could I have many?* Kyle thought of the old saying that one shouldn't judge a book by its cover, But *If my cover, or shadow, reflects a cowboy today, maybe those other shadows could show me what I'm capable of too. John talked about growing wisdom; maybe Nancy used different words, but I think the meaning was precisely the same. They were both talking about some external feature that could never display the growth of wisdom within. This shadow might convey the idea of a cowboy today, but it could never reveal the growing wisdom within, so it would seem the image is nothing more than a facade.* Kyle looked at Dingo with this scholarly understanding, but Dingo just returned his gaze and seemed utterly content with her shadow of a dog. Kyle couldn't help laughing at his seriousness while visualizing his rocket approaching.

cowboy hat shadow

one leg crosses over

natural statue

About a month after Kyle started, the area received unexpected rain for a few days in a row. The sandy washes were about to become impossible for any vehicle to cross, so everyone vacated the ranch before it got so bad that they couldn't get home. Kevin, Dingo, and Kyle were left behind on the high ground with the horses for a few days.

Kyle spent most of those days reading his newest book in the bunkhouse. He paused between two chapters to look over at Dingo, who was tracking a fly as it buzzed around her. Annoyed, she simply caught it in her mouth with a snap. Kyle thought she was just lucky with that one, but moments later, she did it again, and then a minute later, another was trapped as her jaws snapped shut. He smiled at this ability and wondered about this dog's other skills that she might not share as he turned back to reading his novel.

The rain came down continuously for three days, and as far as Kyle could see, the desert had been replaced by lakes and rivers. He thought about how hot and arid it had been just a few days before and how the surrounding land was beautiful but dreadfully inhospitable. Even though the land seemed to be covered in water now, a few weeks later, the land returned to what Kyle remembered the desert looking like in picture books. But for those few weeks, Kyle enjoyed watching Dingo frolic as she played in the new rivers around the rocks. The ranch was backed up against millions of acres of public land so she could play in a huge backyard. As Kyle opened the bunkhouse door, Dingo stepped into a canine playground filled with sights, sounds, and smells any dog might find mesmerizing.

Kyle understood he was being taught to live, laugh, and be curious by example. Dingo seemed like an "old soul" to Kyle, but Dingo also seemed to take pleasure in little events. She looked happy as she played with a stick or treasuring a scrap of horse hoof after the blacksmith left. In these timeless moments, Kyle couldn't help but think; *Probably there's just some simple meaning in daily life that I fail to grasp. And here I am, 47 years old, going back into the world on a journey that might not lead anywhere, searching for something I think would be significant.*

Kyle composed a haiku, contemplating a ranch dog in the pasture with the horses.

brown horse eats green grass

white dog eats apples from horse

both enjoy meadow

As the temperature went up, the guests didn't visit as much. Some days would be very quiet, and everyone would get busy with the abundance of chores that don't fit into daily work on a dude ranch, but one red-hot day Kevin had talked the ranch handyman into bringing his mini cannon to the deserted ranch. Kyle thought that by "mini," the others meant he was bringing some kind of desk ornament, but this "mini" fired a lead ball about 3 inches in diameter. The mini cannon required two men to position it, so it was not small! Kevin helped to load it and suggested a sandy hill to shoot at. Dingo seemed to know what would happen and casually wandered off into town.

After a few minutes of loading, aiming, and talking about the possible outcome, the cannon was fired at the side of a hill about 100 yards away. With a colossal BOOM and cloud of smoke, it probably created an enormous furrow in the ground. Everyone wanted to see the deformed lead ball from the cannon, so this was Kyle's chance to search for the gold in that conquistador's cave and that cannonball at the same time.

Kyle hiked the hillside with Dingo trailing behind for almost an hour, looking for the furrow in the sand created by the cannonball. Not finding any sign of the cannonball, they turned toward the conquistador's cave. As they approached the cave from above, Kyle grabbed onto a bush to lower himself, but Dingo just sat nearby on a boulder to watch. Once down, Kyle was level with the entrance and could almost see in, but there were dark shadows. He was only about 15 feet away, but that 15-foot span was covered with loose sand and small stone lying on that steep slope. Kyle guessed he could leap about 8 feet and then maybe scramble the other 6 or 7 feet to something secure. If he guessed wrong, though, he'd have that inevitable 200-foot drop ahead of him. At that thought, he turned around and grabbed the bush to steady his climb over the rock and continue searching for the cannonball. Kyle thought with a shrug, *Maybe being rich from that conquistador's treasure isn't as important as being able to grow my wisdom some more.*

That evening he visited Kevin's camp to tell him about the failed assault on the conquistador's cave. The two stood pointing at the cave and the prominent landmarks from below where the approach looks deceptively easy. Dingo stepped up on her flat rock while Kyle and Kevin talked. After the sun went down, Kyle wandered the short trail back to the bunkhouse with Dingo.

This area is so fascinating. As Dingo and I were out walking around rattlesnakes and looking at the rocks in the sand, I was astonished to think that these things probably looked identical a hundred years ago. It probably looks like it did way back, so the stories I hear could be from last week or a hundred years ago. Time doesn't seem to move very much out here, and it seems evolution happens very slowly around here, which makes me think that the flexible thinking Nancy was talking about would probably not fit out here. Flexible thinking might even be an evolutionary step that would be frowned upon out here.

The more I examine the relationship between this reality, which I think is totally concrete, and my dream state, which tends to be somewhat whimsical and fuzzy, the more I see fewer elements that make this reality separate. The vision I had about the lightness of cotton fiber is whimsical and definitely fuzzy, and it occurred in this reality that I thought was totally "concrete." The idea that Dingo possibly has some significant information to give me would also be regarded as a very fuzzy thought.

It's frustrating that I always seem to be looking at the same thing; I see it from different perspectives, making me think I haven't seen it before. I keep hearing the same wise words endlessly repeated by various people, but wisdom and grace are always displayed by Dingo. I'm disturbed by the idea that I should have been able to achieve wisdom simply because I can think. Thinking should place me above dogs, but grace seems out of reach for me.

While helping Kevin clean the barn the following day, Kyle asked, "Have you read the book 'Zen Mind'?"

Kevin said, "Sure! I know that book. I've had a few copies over the years. The author was talking about Zen Buddhism. I feel like the meaning of that one is that most of the suffering we encounter maybe comes from something within us that we learned and not being able to approach each event as if it were the first time. I'm guessing that's why those Zen guys spend so much time meditating. I think some of the things we learned could talk to us through that subtle whisper and be invalid information."

"What do you mean?"

"If that subtle whisper tells me that rain is bad, I might suffer when it rains, but with meditation, maybe I could discern that subtle whisper and see that a rainy day is just another day that I might enjoy, like the first time I did." With a wink, Kevin added, "I love rain, by the way, but you see what I mean."

Kyle smiled, thinking, *I'm kinda surprised to find someone out here who is also fond of that book because it would require very fuzzy thinking to uncover what the author may have been pointing at. Maybe the grace I see Kevin doing with the truck and animals comes from this flexible thinking that Nancy was talking about, so perhaps it does fit in out here.*

Kevin pointed at Dingo. "Take her, for example. It doesn't seem those subtle whispers slow her down at all. If something looks like it'll bring her joy in this moment, she goes for it."

Kyle focused his gaze on Kevin. "But don't you think dogs and people are different? We could evaluate the situation before jumping in?"

Kevin leaned his rake by the door and turned to look at Kyle. "Sometimes, maybe, but I think humans do it way too often. Like the author mentioned in his book, having that beginner's mind might be challenging." Kevin pointed to Dingo again, "But when we see someone else living joyfully and with that beginner's mind, maybe we'll find something wrong with them or decide they didn't evaluate entirely. If we don't lock ourselves up with thinking, evaluating, and weighing every situation, we might live a more joyful and simple life. There's something totally right about following your joy, like Dingo." Kevin shrugged, saying, "Maybe that's an oversimplified understanding, but it's what I got from that book."

Kyle exclaimed, "I like that understanding. It's more like he was talking directly to me. No matter how much I studied that book, I couldn't understand the concepts. I thought it was just too deep, or the author had too much cleverness for me ever to grasp what he was saying." Kyle looked towards Dingo and vowed to be more like her because she probably already knew this truth. Kyle pondered the wisdom of keeping your focus on your joy and thought, *Dingo always seems gracefully, keeping her joy in focus.*

A few days later, as Kyle walked behind Dingo up one of the many trails on the ranch, she stopped mid-stride and looked toward the horizon as if she'd heard something. Kyle looked that way and saw nothing but remembered being on the beach with Dingo and realizing it was time to travel. Kyle thought with amazement, *She really uses this listening thing.* With the temperature climbing and fewer guests coming to the ranch, the other wranglers could do Kyle's chores, so the next time he talked to Kevin, he told him it was time for him to leave.

Kevin said, "I'll certainly miss your visits to my camper and our talks, but believe me, I know; when it's time, it's time!" Dingo had stepped up on her flat rock and pointing at her, Kevin said, "If it's okay, I'll grab my camera so I can have a photo of her on her rock."

Kyle turned to look at her, "Absolutely! I think she'd love to be photographed."

Kevin went inside to find his camera, and Kyle turned to look at Dingo, thinking, *I wonder why she picked that rock? Maybe it gives her a better view of the desert, or perhaps she can hear more up there.* With a shrug, he thought, *Maybe I'll never know what she sees or hears.*

When Kevin returned, Kyle asked Dingo to look toward the camera, and she gently reached out a paw to touch Kyle's hand, and Kevin snapped a photo just then.

In the twilight, Dingo followed Kyle back to the bunkhouse. The pair started to settle in for the evening, but Kyle kept pondering Dingo's reaction to being photographed and could imagine his spaceship making many orbits. He contemplated making a haiku and saw his spaceship immediately alter its course. Kyle smiled at his observation while reaching for a pen.

I asked her to pose

lightly touching my hand

with paw in answer

9 Increase

Kyle kept thinking about that conversation with Kevin as he left the ranch a few days later. *It seems that things keep repeating. I feel like everything is just one thing and keeps showing up for me in different forms. There is something very similar in how nobody could transfer wisdom and Dingo being in silence.*

Kyle and Dingo were walking north on the road when they came upon an older white van with Idaho plates parked in the breakdown lane. Pete introduced himself from under the hood, offering a ride as soon as he got the van started again. Kyle accepted, saying, "We'd love a ride. My brother is gonna meet me up north, and we probably wouldn't make it walking. Can I help you at all?"

"No. It's an easy fix, and I'll be done in a sec."

The van was running a few minutes later, and when they were about 20 miles north, Pete said to Kyle, "I'm a nomad, too. I've been living in this van for about two years, wandering around the U.S., and I move whenever the mood strikes me." Pete thought he had found a kindred spirit and shared, "I've been coast to coast three times." Kyle felt unimpressed but asked, "What inspires your travels?" Pete listed many instances where rules or laws made no sense to him and made it hard for nomadic people to exist. It seemed to Kyle that Pete was on a mission to prove those rules or laws wrong. Kyle thought *This struggling energy could be put into something else. Being distracted by and shining your flashlight on what you see as wrong would take as much energy as shining your flashlight on what you see as joyful or right. I remember my friends trying to convince me that this path was wrong, so I guess anyone can take whatever path they choose and shine their flashlight where ever they want.*

Kyle and Dingo rode north in the van, and he was more aware of Dingo as Nancy had told him to watch. He observed Dingo moving around Pete. She certainly didn't avoid him, but she also didn't seem to have a strong desire to be around him like she did with Jeb. Kyle thought dogs seemed to immediately sense if you're someone they should buddy up with, steer clear of, or altogether bypass. *How cool would it be to have if I had that superpower? Seeing through to the being beneath the surface would be beneficial because I'd save all that energy when I meet someone new. How do dogs do that monumental task in every moment with utter ease?* Kyle looked again at Dingo with envy. *This may be part of the beginner's mind I was discussing with Kevin 'cause whenever somebody tells me about wisdom, I see Dingo's already doing it.* He was starting to appreciate the ease with which Dingo moved through life.

Pete told Kyle, "I've got some people to visit and some errands to do, but I can drop you off in the center of town a few hours up the road and pick you up when I start heading to Idaho in a couple of weeks."

"That would be great! We could rest up." They exchanged phone numbers before Pete dropped them off.

Kyle relaxed under a tree and watched Dingo play in the park near where Pete had let them off. Dingo played for a while but stopped and was having some exchange with a person in the park. They both walked up to Kyle to rest in the shade of the tree. This new person chatted with Kyle about many things, like preserving a good diet and protecting your mental health on the road. Kyle's new friend informed him of a kind of monastery near them that would feed travelers. It was called an ashram, and the spiritual leader would give a talk after the meals so you could receive great food and feed your mind all at once. Kyle got directions to the ashram from his new friend and started hiking that way with Dingo. He found a great spot and put up his tent on the way.

Kyle had what he felt was a colossal burden, and maybe the ashram was just the place to provide him with insight into this burden and perhaps give him a new understanding of his journey. *Maybe a new understanding is just the thing I need to give my journey a purpose.* Kyle would seek out the wisest person at the ashram and present this dilemma.

Leaving Dingo to watch over the camp, Kyle continued to the ashram and, as he got near, noticed people gathering outside.

After a meal of delicious steamed rice and curried beets, Kyle was invited to sit with the group to listen to that night's topic for contemplation. The Swami started the conversation by presenting an idea, speaking about it briefly, and then asking the group for thoughts. Next, he read a bit from a book the Swami plucked from the shelf. It had a picture of what looked to be a Japanese guy on the back, which Kyle could see from where he was sitting. Maybe the author was a Buddhist monk or a Catholic priest, but it seemed the notion behind this discourse was not a sermon on any specific tradition but an understanding that the truth is for anyone to discover along any path.

The Swami summarized what he'd read to the group as having to do something with the idea of increase. "It often seems we won't even participate in an activity unless we think there's going to be some increase."

Kyle couldn't help but feel like the Swami was speaking about Kyles' journey. *Is he reading my mind?* Kyle wanted to ask the Swami privately, but this was perfect timing. Kyle told the group about the trip he was on and wanting to have some meaning to the whole thing. He presented a question to the group and the Swami. "Is wanting some meaning for my journey the same as wanting money or fame?" The Swami thanked Kyle. "That's a wonderful question." Someone else in the group drew a metaphoric parallel between the path life takes and the *simple* journey Kyle might be on. Swami thanked that person for the contribution and said, "Yes, indeed, that could be the case." Turning toward Kyle, "But any return you seek on that path could be an increase. You're faced with continuing your journey without an obvious increase or discontinuing it because it has no increase you can detect. The trap of doing anything with the idea of increase is that the increase becomes the primary focus of the doing. Hypothetically, in Kyle's case, let's say he's looking for an increase of $100,000. The journey won't be successful if that amount is not met, but the only one that can judge if they're on the right path is the person walking the walk. Of course, the increase he's thinking of could be more complicated than mere money, but whether we want money or insight, the process of seeking a return is the same. The question we must ask ourselves is, is it possible to make a choice without any deciding based on increase? What if the choice based on increase actually rendered the selection irrelevant."

Swami talked for almost an hour more, but Kyle was too lost in his own thoughts to follow and just sat there till the group dispersed. *How can I do anything without some thought of increase?* Kyle shook his head slowly. *This is the same idea I had about wisdom. As wisdom is being spoken, it's turned into gibberish and probably doesn't even resemble wisdom. The decision becomes dubious if a choice is made based on increase or a wished-for outcome, which brings me back to just watching Dingo doing grace all the time.* Kyle smiled at the simplicity of the thought of having only one choice to choose.

As Kyle would probably speak with the Swami again, he decided to reflect on his possible thoughts of increase later back at his camp. Swamiji's information made Kyle think of the many possible interpretations of increase, yet one was most prominent in his mind. *Should I continue the journey without any increase? Would striving for some increase put me on an incorrect path, and could any planned increase automatically halt my evolution? Too many thoughts flow through my mind, and meanings evaporate, even in the very straightforward and simple haiku.*

the Swamiji talks

about philosophy but

most of all loving

The next day Kyle showed up back at the ashram more for the talk than that delicious meal. Kyle was again invited to sit with the group after the meal. The Swami plucked another book off the shelf. Kyle noticed that these books didn't come from one group talking about the benefits of their school of thought but were varied and only had wisdom in common. He had looked through most of the books and recognized the one chosen for tonight. It was a light blue book with translations from the ancient language of Sanskrit about yoga. Kyle was stunned as the Swami read a passage about the fear of death. He had been considering his fears the moment he walked through the door tonight, and he remembered talking about fears with Lucy months ago. The Swami spoke about how instinct plays into our skills as we reincarnate and then asked if anyone had anything to add or had any questions.

A thought occurred to Kyle, and he raised a hand to get Swami's attention. He asked if he had died before and been reincarnated, why would he be afraid to die again? Swami said, "Usually, people forget about being reborn and just focus on the many things they want to achieve." After a moment of thought, Kyle questioned by saying, "Then it's actually a fear of life."

Swami said, "You could say fear of death is a fear of not having lived. If a person has some destination in mind, fear of the ending brings thoughts of not achieving that particular destination while living. You remember we were talking about increase?" That statement made Kyle's head swim, and he told Swami he wasn't following. Swami said, "Okay, let me say it this way. If you had some goal to get to before you die and understand that death is just around the corner for you, you might feel like the goal has become unreachable. It's unreachable only because you forgot about your eventual reincarnation. You could imagine it as simply going around, over and over."

Once again, Swami talked with the group for another hour, but Kyle was lost and didn't follow anything more. Just as Kyle was about to leave that evening, the Swami caught his attention and asked him to wait.

As the group was scattering after the talk, one of Swami's students asked him a quiet question, but Swami was soon done conversing with his student and, turning to Kyle, said, "I was thinking about your walking, and you may want to try this. It's simply walking at a slightly slower pace. You'd do this for maybe a 10-minute stretch. It's great: when you have some goal in mind and find yourself walking a little faster, try walking at half that rate. You will get there, but going slower may just put that goal in perspective. Even if there is no goal, find the 10 minutes to practice daily." To demonstrate, the Swami walked across the room at an average walking speed and returned at half that rate, placing his feet very deliberately. "Focus attention on the feel of earth on your foot. Feel your heel really making contact, then the middle part of your foot, the ball of your foot, and finally your toes." Swamiji pointed at Kyle's foot, saying, "I hope you can use that."

"I can, and thank you for the meals."

The Swami rested a hand on Kyle's shoulder, "And don't let the thoughts distract you too much."

Kyle scrunched his eyebrows together as a question.

"The thoughts don't deserve as much attention as you give them. They might even give you false information or tell you to do something you wouldn't normally do. When the thoughts come, try the walking as I showed you."

Kyle nodded. He held up his index finger, "Speaking of thoughts; there's one that seems to keep hounding me. A friend tried to explain emptiness, and many times since, I think I know what it is and have found it, but then I realize I don't have any idea what emptiness is."

The Swami nodded, saying, "Emptiness can be a tough one." He paused to take a slow breath, "Rationally speaking, emptiness is where everything comes from and can be traced back to. But that explanation will only give you another thought to think, so know that by doing things more intentionally, like that walking meditation I showed you, or taking time out to breathe like you were talking about, the experience of emptiness will simply arrive. Thoughts just seem to function to push that experience farther away. So when you notice thoughts have come, try those practices."

Kyle nodded partial understanding and vaguely associated his thoughts with his rocket ship. He thanked the Swami again and bid him farewell. Wandering back to his campsite, he noticed the double rainbow over the mountains of Sedona. It would be dry where Kyle camped, so he didn't even bother setting up his tent. As darkness would soon be closing in around him, he spread the fabric of his tent on the ground. Kyle dug through his bag for the journal by the light of his headlamp.

I've had very little interaction with people that have devoted their lives to discovering the genuineness of human events. What I understand and what they actually intend may be two different things, kinda like when Swamiji showed me that walking meditation technique. I think he called it a meditation though I've never seen people meditating while moving. He probably knows what effect it would have, and later, he did tell me about not paying so much attention to my thoughts. They must be connected. It seems all the thoughts and experiences I thought would bring me wisdom were all the time actually pushing wisdom farther away. It will take me forever to attain any kind of wisdom, thinking thoughts, and struggling to have more experiences. Perhaps the Swami pointed me in the general direction so I might discover the essence of my thoughts for myself.

I wonder if hearing wisdom from someone wise would make the information useless and cancel the possibility of me actually seeing the wisdom. Maybe that's why Dingo points me to silence. I feel there must be something significant I'm missing. I imagine myself on the first rung of a ladder, struggling to rise higher. I think there's some basic idea that I fail to grasp, even though it may be presented to me many times and in many different forms. Maybe the Swami points to the experience of that basic idea that everyone might climb to the top rung of the ladder and, from there, soar away. Months ago, I remember writing about the wish that my friends would have said, "See how high you can fly and tell me what you discover," but even though I was given the formula for discovery by

the Swami and I got repeated signals from Dingo, I doubt whether I can even get to the first rung of that ladder. Wisdom may forever escape my grasp.

Kyle was packing the last of his things the following day in the dawn. He looked toward the gray horizon where the sun would be shining in a half hour and realized he never had any need to wake Dingo as she always seemed to know when it was time to go. The pair walked together out of the campsite north. Kyle felt genuinely gloomy as he followed Dingo on the side of the road toward Flagstaff. He wanted something to look forward to; an end to this wandering or even a friend to welcome the two into their home. He guessed that's what the Swami meant about an increase. He felt desperate because he lacked safety or security on this journey.

I wonder why I keep recreating my friends' interrogations from back home. Maybe they were right in telling me that I shouldn't travel, and I was just overly confident back then about giving up home as part of my journey. Today I miss that comfy chair in my living room and that group of aircraft mechanics I worked with. Even the people I found unpleasant, I look back on affectionately today. Perhaps it was beyond me, at the time, to discover any comfort or safety in that group, but I was part of a team that spoke the same language and performed the same tasks. I gave that up, and now I miss being part of something like that. I don't think anyone feels as alone as me. I feel emotionally exhausted. Wandering from town to town will not increase the funds in my checking account. Kyle's shoulders slumped, and something soft poked his leg just then. Turning, he saw it was Dingo nudging him with her nose. Making eye contact with Dingo, Kyle knew he had been lost in thought, and the two continued walking, this time with Kyle focusing on his breathing.

Kyle noticed a store selling used books next to the library and, leaving his backpack with Dingo at the door, went in to browse. He thought maybe a new book to read might lighten his mood. Kyle thought about filling the emptiness with something and decided his reading couldn't possibly prevent examining his emptiness, but that thought would have to wait for another time.

The person by the door asked if they could point him in any particular direction, and he said with a smile, "I don't know exactly what I'm looking for." Kyle held up his most recent books for the person to see, saying, "I have a couple of books I'd like to trade." The front door person replied, "Wonderful, just leave them on the desk here and look around." He let the quiet lead him around the shelves, and soon he discovered the book with the blue feather that Nancy had mentioned. Kyle didn't bother reading the back cover, as always, before deciding to buy it. As he talked to the person about the book exchange, he remembered another book he wanted to look at and described what he was seeking. The book Pete had mentioned about the old rancher in the desert was quickly pointed out by the person at the door for Kyle to retrieve. Putting the two books in his backpack, he shouldered the new load, and he and Dingo continued north.

Kyle noticed the creek running next to them as they walked and looked for a place to rest away from the road. He saw a spot out of the sun just around the next turn of the road. He wandered to the spot next to the tree that hung over the creek and swung his pack down. Sitting on his pack and draping an affectionate arm around Dingo, they both gazed at the babbling brook. Kyle acknowledged to himself his fear of being alone but was grateful that he could feel warmth for Dingo.

Pete caught up with them a few days later at a natural food store in Flagstaff on his way farther north. The three were soon settled in Pete's van and headed north, and Kyle said, "I'm glad you caught up with us 'cause Dingo is a little foot-sore today and limping."

Pete vaguely nodded and said, "Sure thing. I'm happy to give you guys a lift."

Kyle could tell Pete was lost in thought because he recognized the same expression Kyle would carry on his face and turned to look at Dingo with an affirmative nod. Dingo was already staring up at Kyle with a somewhat knowing expression.

Pete explained out of the blue, "There's another freedom stealing law be passed about drifters I heard about back in town."

Kyle nodded at Pete's explanation but more at his inner confirmation of Pete's state of mind. *Freedom from something is not the same as true freedom. If someone is genuinely free, they have no interest in the idea of 'being free' or in complaining about some organization 'stealing' some freedom. Removing some binding or handcuffs doesn't assure your freedom; it just means you're not bound.*

freedom from something

is not actual freedom

bindings merely removed

A few hours later, Pete pointed to the sun approaching the western horizon saying, "I'm sure there are some great places to camp out there, so help me keep an eye out for a forest road or maybe even a jeep trail that leads off into the forest." A couple of miles later, Kyle pointed through the windshield. "How 'bout that one there?" Pete started to slow the van down. "Perfect. That one looks great." In about 10 minutes, Pete was settling the van in its spot for the night under some trees and next to some brush. Kyle opened the door when the van was stopped, saying, "There you go, Dingo." She leaped out and disappeared into the brush. Kyle watched as she investigated the area and then turned his attention to helping Pete unload his van.

Kyle unfolded a chair to watch the setting sun when all the camping supplies were unloaded. Dingo found him sitting quietly when she returned from her scouting trip. She seemed to smile, and her tail waved when she came around the van and saw him. Kyle noticed her approach and smiled as Dingo sat down next to him. He focused on her and said, "There you are!" Dingo seemed to be staring into his eyes, and she reached out a paw to gently rest on his knee. Kyle had never seen her reach out a paw for anything, and he wondered what she might be saying. Was it something like, "Time for dinner," or maybe "I can see what you're thinking is not a joyful thought?" Whatever it was, he couldn't make it out and felt grief well up in his chest because he could never share even the most basic ideas with her. If it were the latter of the two statements she was making, he would certainly agree with her and choose to focus on all the wonderful things he was doing and seeing right now.

Later as the three relaxed around a tiny campfire, Kyle said, "We appreciate all the rides. It saved us a lot of walking."

Pete nodded, saying, "No problem. It was my pleasure; I was glad for the company. Do you have any idea how long you'll travel or where you're going?"

Kyle stared into the fire, shrugged, and, petting Dingo said, "Nope: not a clue."

"That's one of the things I love about being a nomad. I never really know where or when I'll go. I can be camped in Utah one night and then in Montana a few nights later. It'll probably be about 2 in the afternoon tomorrow when we get to the spot where I'll drop you off. It'll be easy for you to catch a ride from there."

There must have been some rain late in the night because the dirt road was muddy and slick. Kyle worried about getting stuck out in the woods but glanced at Dingo sitting gracefully near. He remembered Lucy talking about finding the real-world benefit and considered the walking meditation he'd do later.

rain makes mud-tires spin

driver tries to find traction

on the road to town

10 Journey till the last step

They passed a mountain as he and Dingo moved farther north toward Kyle's brother.

rocky mountain top

spewed many fiery stones

volcano now rests

The pair entered the next small town from the south, and walking along the sidewalk, someone pointed at Dingo and told Kyle there's a really nice dog park nearby. Assuming Dingo needed to interact with other dogs, Kyle wandered in the direction the stranger had steered him. As they went through the gate at the dog park, Kyle watched as Dingo transformed into a social butterfly. *Maybe she's using precisely the etiquette expected as she approaches each dog. Dingo employs a slightly different tactic for her greeting. I think it's amazing that she knows precisely what each dog expects before she even approaches.* Kyle counted about ten dogs as Dingo made her way to the final dog on the outskirts of the pack. He noticed that this last dog had lost one of its legs. Dingo drifted over, licked the dog's mouth, and rolled over on the ground.

The owner of that dog introduced herself with some fictional and whimsical name that maybe she thought better described her mystical essence, pointing at Dingo, "That's typical submissive behavior." Kyle nodded as she launched into a description of alpha and omega pack behavior. Kyle nodded again as he looked at Dingo and the three-legged dog playing together without any sort of discrimination. *Humans might instantaneously regard a being that's missing a leg as inferior. Still, Dingo, and the three-legged dog, don't seem to consider each other alpha, beta, or omega dogs, and I wonder if this mystical woman is telling me what she's read or maybe what she's heard. It's evident that something far greater may be occurring between these two dogs that words might fail to describe. Maybe we can never know what these dogs feel, think, or see. I think it's just another demonstration of grace.* With a wave goodbye to the mystical woman, Kyle turned towards the exit. He didn't need to check if Dingo followed him; he knew she was trailing him as they'd done for miles. *It's probably not so much that I know she's there; I think she follows my emerging grace.* As the pair reached the gate, Kyle held it open for her as Dingo self-assuredly strolled past.

They made their way through town and farther north, where they'd meet Kyle's brother. A couple of days later, they wandered into town for breakfast, and Kyle looked around the little café patio where he'd meet his brother and wondered if he'd even recognize Daniel after these six years. Daniel strolled in about 10 minutes into Kyle's second cup of coffee and was slightly surprised to see Dingo. "You have a dog?" he said with a warm smile. He said, "That's pretty cool." He extended a hand for Dingo to sniff, and she gratefully accepted a pet under her chin. Daniel hugged his brother, and they exchanged the remark, "It's so good to see you." After breakfast, they talked over another cup of coffee, but Kyle felt at a loss and was totally confused when instructed by Daniel to tell him everything that was happening. Kyle started talking about how Dingo found him and the wise things he heard while traveling. Finally, Kyle spoke about what Swami said regarding fear and how he could practically read his mind in the group talks, which led to disclosing his fear of this endless journey while not having a purpose.

Daniel put a crooked philosophical smile on his face. He said, "It may seem obvious, but If the journey is not embarked on, no destination will ever be reached, and if a journey is started, but no destination is ever reached, the steps on that journey will make absolutely no sense. Have you ever been partway somewhere and forgotten what you set out to do? The steps then made no sense. No journey has a fixed number of steps; sometimes, you must travel to understand why you're traveling. Maybe you even uncover a destination on your way."

"Some folks may be told you not even to start the journey, but they weren't called to journey, and so their advice on your path is utterly useless." Daniel pointed at Kyle, saying, "You must go boldly in some direction even if you rationalize it to be wrong because life will eventually choose for you if you don't, and you may not like where you end up."

Kyle puckered his brow in question.

Daniel explained, "What I'm saying is the significance you were talking about before is never attained in achieving some dream but rather in the way you boldly move through life on the way to that dream. Imagine the significance you'd feel by announcing your path to the universe instead of going wherever the breeze pushes you." Pointing again at Kyle for emphasis, "I say simply choose a direction and claim that path."

Kyle remembered all the advice he had received in his hometown and questions about where he might be headed. Did the universe spit Kyle out, saying, "I'm not done with you yet"? Kyle wondered if some reason for his being out here escaped him. The Swami in Sedona seemed to be talking about changing some focal point. What if the universe had been directing him to watch something close by, but he kept missing it? He thought, *How long should I keep wandering? If this journey has no fixed number of steps, as Daniel said, I might wander forever.*

One evening Kyle was reading his most recent book, and before turning a page, he glanced at the sleeping Dingo. Her feet twitched, and a wave of nostalgia washed over him as he recalled all the miles they covered together. *I wonder if she was sent to escort me on this journey because I wouldn't have had grace displayed. My attachment to this dog had grown into something more than just love. Is it feeling a dog's unconditional love, or maybe I feel something more profound, like respecting a fellow traveler?*

Kyle looked forward to having morning coffee and conversation with his brother even though he understood that philosophical concepts are sometimes just a tricky play on words, not the wisdom Dingo displayed. He felt cheered by seeing a familiar face every day.

That evening, Daniel told Kyle about a great trail he'd like to take them to in the hills above town.

Daniel, Kyle, and Dingo hiked a little way apart from each other. Sunlight filtered through the leaves, creating dancing shadows on the trail in front of Kyle. A creek ran below the trail that Dingo crossed and re-crossed many times. Daniel hiked ahead and just out of sight, so Kyle naturally fell into his subtle thoughts and allowed his rocket to make its unnecessary orbits.

After many miles of travel, Kyle had become accustomed to his hiking staff, and he'd added a bell to the lanyard threaded through some holes so it rang every time the stick touched the ground. He heard the sound of the clip-clop of his footsteps and fancied this new ringing sound might signify his ability to choose a unique path. His thoughts turned to the new information he was reading. If the author of his new book is accurate about our beliefs being obtained from someone else, those beliefs don't belong to us. He felt the reason for his overwhelming anxiety was that a part of his being was no longer content with walking someone else's path. If that is true, then what we believe is not graceful and can't be our path. The thought surprised him that the wisdom and grace he had discovered might always have been with him all along, but he missed it because he wasn't on his own path. He looked around at the trees with that understanding and took a moment to breathe.

Kyle looked at Dingo as more than a friend and had followed her lead as a master many times. Dingo made these complicated ideas look so simple. Kyle smiled at the thought, *I've come up with some really complex ideas and ways to implement grace, but it always seemed much more straightforward trying her approach. Yes, she is a fellow traveler, but I somehow feel the awe and respect usually given to a wise teacher.* With that newfound idea and understanding, he could always rely on her to show him the most straightforward way; Kyle felt at ease in the world and could continue traveling forever. Maybe in time, Kyle thought, I'll even possess that wisdom and perhaps become like the ancient masters I've read about.

He looked around to share that moment with Dingo, but she was nowhere to be seen. Fear filled his every cell, and he became breathless. Kyle turned fully around to check the path behind him and call her name, but it occurred to him that he'd never needed to call her to come as she'd always just been where she was designed to be. A lump of fear formed in his throat, making it difficult to be heard, so he started looking behind bushes, trees, and rocks that might conceal her. Trying frantically to find her, he asked himself questions like, *Had she found someone's company she liked better? Maybe I was somehow unkind to her?* Kyle had been distracted thinking about the ancient master within and thought, *No ancient master would run willy-nilly through the forest trying desperately to find their dog. I doubt that any of the ancient masters even have a dog. What was I thinking?* Kyle shook his head in disbelief at himself, *It's amazing I was thinking I had any kind of wisdom.* Kyle jogged to the other side where he had last seen Dingo playing in the creek. Saddened at the thought of being alone, Kyle shuffled back to the path and built a small marker with rocks to help when he brought Daniel back to search for Dingo.

He hurried up the path and, about 20 minutes later, found Daniel resting on a rock. Kyle immediately fell into what he thought was a heart-wrenching story of loss. At this point, Kyle was beside himself with worry, but Daniel just raised a hand to pause the frantic story. Then, with a questioning look, he pointed through the trees, and Kyle looked in the direction indicated. He nearly yelled out, "DINGO!" Kyle's shoulders fell at the same time his heart soared.

Daniel had not seen Kyle this out of sorts and asked him, "What brought that on?"

Kyle thought back to just 30 minutes ago and could only say, "I thought I'd lost her and would never see her again." Even at the time, he knew there were lots more to it, but Kyle just shrugged as he turned to Dingo. He walked over and sat beside her, draping an arm around her.

Kyle asked her quietly, "What was that?" He felt odd addressing a dog so frankly. Maybe even more peculiar than he felt on the ranch when considering emotional support dogs. This was way beyond idle chatter with a pet. Kyle was addressing Dingo as a mentor, and as soon as he did, the idea came to him that his overthinking things would probably lead to his being endlessly disturbed and losing any grace he had discovered. Kyle had given up his grace in a flash because he falsely believed his wisdom and grace existed in another. Kyle looked at his arm draped over Dingo's neck and asked, "Dingo, was the lesson about acting through grace? How can someone do grace when they're terrified?" Somehow Kyle knew the answer would come because he had been courageous enough to ask.

He wandered over to Daniel and said with a smile in his voice, "This dog is my Co-pilot! I guess I thought I couldn't go on without my co-pilot."

Daniel shook his head in disbelief and continued walking. "I don't understand your attachment to that dog."

Daniel, Kyle, and Dingo spent most every other afternoon exploring the trails around town, followed by an evening meal at the café in town. Kyle figured they were doing what all brothers do; still, he felt some significant piece might be missing. Daniel went home a week later and left Kyle to continue his journey. Though Daniel gave Kyle a hearty blessing, Kyle knew something had been withheld. Kyle couldn't place exactly what it was, but he thought, *Maybe my journey is separating me and moving me farther away from family and friends. I didn't mind leaving my friends back home, but somehow, I didn't associate separating from friends the same as separating from family. What if this journey continues for the rest of my life...or longer? Moving around like Pete without any connection or a place in the world terrifies me. I may never have family or friends again.* Looking at Dingo with a smile, Kyle thought, *But my new family might have already started with Dingo, and the road could be our home. Maybe my wanderings seem pointless, but I should have some confidence that this is all orchestrated.*

However, standing next to his tent that evening, Kyle was doubtfully staring at the lights from the cars on the road about ¼ mile away. The taillights just reminded him that his brother had left him behind without a backward glance. Maybe Daniel felt like his brother knew exactly what he was doing, or perhaps he was too tired to interject. But standing next to his tent, Kyle felt utterly alone and without faith in himself or the universe. Kyle thought back to the T.V. show about the wandering Kung Fu guy. It seemed to Kyle that the simplicity of that journey had nothing in common with his, and he wanted nothing more than an end to this wandering. *If only there were some spectacular reason for my journey, like that old T.V. show of the kung-fu monk.* He shrugged and turned to climb in with the sleeping Dingo and find his journal.

I was thinking about Daniel's statement regarding my friends not being called to travel. They probably wouldn't have any concept or understanding of my journey. Traveling is only half of the equation because if you travel with only the destination in mind, you might miss the journey's point or witness something significant along the way. There is a statement I read some years ago. It says, "That which you are seeking is causing you to seek," and I thought for the longest time that statement was just "mumbo-jumbo,"; but now I understand that seeking does prevent finding because if one is seeking, they would see only the thing they are watching for and nothing else. It's like my spaceship going around endlessly, never reaching any destination and failing to see anything along the path. So, I'll never find any grace if I'm seeking it. As Daniel said, maybe it's kind of like my traveling to discover why I have to travel. I might never discover the reason for my travel if I don't travel. I thought Daniel was playing with words to make them twist, but there is intelligence in what he said. Discovering the essence of something by committing to it...and doing it boldly couldn't hurt either! I wasn't sure about doing grace boldly, as I thought the two were opposites, but now I see they aren't at all opposites. I see grace as wisdom in action. I can't believe that wisdom and doing grace are so simple that they can be accessed through silence. All the questions I've agonized over could have been solved by simply accessing the wisdom that has always been in me by creating a silent place. I thought wisdom was contained in the people I met, like John and the Swami, but they only talked about the wisdom that Dingo is forever demonstrating.

Dingo seems to be the best model for me to do silence. Probably that horrible fear I felt in losing Dingo today was just me believing I can't do grace, but some other being can. When I thought I had lost her, there was just fear of loss for me and no space for truth. The lesson, I guess Dingo wanted me to see, was that I don't have to go running after wisdom because I have it. I'd read the wise words of some masters and believed that, somehow, those masters were gifted and that I could focus on them, but I never saw the simplicity of their message; they were always pointing to grace and wisdom. Dingo was silently pointing all along. I'm reminded of that trite saying about dogs: ' Please let me be the person my dog thinks I am, and I'm pretty sure Dingo knows who I am and what I'm capable of.

I remember Lucy pointing out that I could either wear myself out in the anxiety of possible failure or simply do grace in every moment. I realize that Dingo is telling me I don't need to wear myself out 'trying.'

concern in her eyes

I ponder what she sees

it must be the stress

Kyle turned out his headlamp and rested back to close his eyes. He rolled over to reach Dingo in the dark. As he rested a hand on her, he felt her slowly breathe in her sleep, and his breathing naturally relaxed and slowed, so he was drawn into his own slumber.

Kyle relaxed outside his tent the next day, reading in the sunlight. Dingo found a great place to snooze and had been napping for a few chapters but woke suddenly with a gathering together of limbs to rise and stare across the trail. Kyle looked over the top of his book in the direction Dingo stared. His human eyes and ears could make nothing out, but Dingo stood rigid, with her ears like radar dishes, rotating minutely to pinpoint something that Kyle could not see. He continued to gaze at what seemed like a peaceful hill across the trail, hoping to see the shadow of some animal slinking its way through the trees. There was another camper 50 yards up the trail, and Kyle saw one ear twitch in that direction before Dingo locked back onto the silence to the east across the path. Kyle could hear that other camper moving around his tent in the morning sun. Kyle felt very slow on the uptake like someone might be trying to explain something to him slowly and in very simple terms. He never saw anything that would attract attention and eventually turned away from the hill, shaking his head in wonder at the supernatural gift of hearing Dingo must have.

Kyle sat down next to Dingo, draping an arm around her, and dug through his pack for the postcard he wanted to send to Eddie. Kyle thought, *Writing a postcard is kind of like making a haiku. There might not be enough space on this card to convey his journey's impact, so maybe I'll just write about finding Dingo and draw a picture.* At the bottom, Kyle signed his name and wrote, 'I wish you were here.'

Kyle turned to look down at Dingo, saying with a longing in his voice, "Sometimes, I wish I was here. I get lost in thought, so thank you for guiding me back."

11 Connection between wisdom/silence/pause

A few weeks of walking brought them through a low pass through the Rockies and over some divide. Kyle looked around at the mountains surrounding them like the rim of a bowl with the tops all white with snow. The lakes they passed were icy cold, and Kyle knelt by one to wash his face as Dingo took a drink.

A couple of days later, the pair was hiking south along a trail that paralleled the road. An hour before sunset, Kyle made camp off the side of the trail to use the remaining light to find things in his pack that he'd maybe packed differently when visiting Daniel. As soon as his hand touched the journal, an idea for a haiku formed in his mind, and Kyle thought back to one of the stories Lucy shared with him about breathing. He looked over at Dingo next to him.

watching the dog breathe

relaxed cycles never stop

un-interrupted

A few days along the trail, Kyle found a path that would get them farther off the road, and the following morning, Kyle and Dingo were at yet a new trailhead. Kyle looked left and right through the trees at all the trails crisscrossing the hills and, finally, checked the map. Of all the trails headed south, the one that took them farthest south added a few miles as it was a bit out of the way. Suddenly Kyle froze with fear looking at the map: He had the feeling he was being watched. Turning slowly around, Kyle saw Dingo had fixed her friendly gaze on him. Flustered, Kyle asked, "What? Did I do something you're looking at?" Dingo's tail swayed in response, and her eyes expressed a definite smile. As he looked closer at her eyes, Kyle felt he was being looked at, like a person gazing at a painting in a museum, maybe searching for some hidden message. Kyle almost expected her to wink. Shrugging, he turned to continue their stroll.

Kyle could see this new path wound its way around to a summit. It looked like a half-mile across to the next summit, and he could see a tiny creek winding its way through the bottom of this canyon. He spent a moment gazing down at the boulders half hidden by the trees on the sides of the creek. Turning to Dingo, "That looks nice; let's go down there." On their way along the path, Dingo went to investigate something off to the right side of the trail, heading uphill toward the summit. Kyle kept walking and, about 10 minutes later, saw Dingo scrambling through the rocks below the path and on the opposite side. Kyle greeted her as she jogged past. "Well, hi! How'd you do that? I'd lose the trail and maybe never find it again if I roamed just a little way off." Looking around to ensure no one was around to hear, he said to Dingo somberly, "I have no idea why I'm walking." With a shrug, he added, "I'm hoping I see something inspiring as I go." Dingo seemed to take no note of what he said but ran ahead to wait at a fork in the trail. When Kyle reached the fork, he took the path to the left that would lead down to that creek. Dingo waited a moment at the fork and then followed.

They reached the creek about an hour later, and after playing with Dingo by the water for a while, Kyle leisurely put up the tent by some trees. After his little camp was set up, Kyle went rest on a rock near the creek. He glanced over at Dingo, and her tail started to sway. Kyle immediately flashed back on his staring at the map and then freezing in terror. *When I turned around, I thought I was going to be met with some life-threatening situation; instead, I saw Dingo staring at me.*

93

He smiled at Dingo, and an expression like he saw while examining the map yesterday crossed her face. *That was probably just a fluke,* he thought and allowed his smile to fade. Dingo returned to her relaxing, and Kyle tried to look at her without being noticed, but in the next moment, her eyes were already opening as soon as his gaze fell on her. A few moments later, Kyle would smile, and her tail would start swaying immediately. He shrugged in response, shook his head as he turned back to the trickle of water, and pondered why he might be out here again.

through the rocks, creek

the sound always the same

but never the same

The next day Dingo watched Kyle pack up the small camp by the creek and then followed him back to the trail. A few hours of hiking brought them to the ridge of a hill. Kyle looked around the forest and picked a new path that would lead downhill to the town.

The pair entered the town a few days later, and passing a coffee shop, Kyle felt like having a bagel and a coffee. He left his pack by a table outside the shop, and as soon as he leaned his walking stick against the wall, Dingo found her place in the shade. Kyle went inside to order a toasted bagel and get his coffee and noticed they had miniature bagels created as dog treats. Kyle returned to the table with his bagel, coffee, and two mini bagel dog treats for Dingo. He wasn't even sure Dingo would appreciate the treats, but he sat down under the awning to enjoy his treat and handed a treat to her. She indulged in the bagel treat and then went into the shade of the awning of the next table. Some people are uncomfortable with a dog near, so Kyle looked at his neighbor, and the other bowed his head a little as a signal that said Dingo was welcome there. His neighbor reached down to pet Dingo asking the usual questions, but he became pretty animated upon discovering their journey's origin. "My name is James." He held a hand out, questioning Kyle, "So you just walked the whole way?"

Kyle shrugged his shoulders. "We got rides some of the way, but mostly we just walked. I'd say we've covered about 1,000 miles so far."

James said, "I thought of doing a journey like that. I always wanted to hike down to Mexico, but I never worked up the courage to go and do it. I always envisioned myself being free if I could do that, but my trip probably would have been more of a little retreat from work. It sounds like yours is more of a grand journey that required a profound commitment, and you probably dared to trust yourself above the arguments and reasonings of others."

James took a sip of his coffee, looked at Kyle, and then, putting his cup down, said, "A friend told me once that courage comes at the price of fear. I've often deliberated on that because I didn't know what he meant." Chuckling, he said, "But now I see it seems too high a price for most people. People probably won't give up thinking that fear is something they should revere and hold onto like it's somehow valuable or proves wisdom is theirs. They might say things like, 'Don't upset the apple cart,' 'You have it pretty good, so don't be so bold,' or 'Tuck tail if that's what's asked of you.' Those words seem like they come from fear, not wisdom. Did they say stuff like that?"

Kyle said, "Yeah, I heard all those arguments and much more. The people I thought would support me seemed to be the very ones who argued the most using that fear-based stuff. I guess they didn't want me to go out and do anything different."

James asked, "Do you mind if I ask about that prosthetic leg? I bet you didn't win many of those arguments with that."

"No. It didn't seem to put my friend's mind at ease, but it was so long ago I've gotten used to it, and I don't even consider it anymore."

"Did it make the trip more challenging?

"It really didn't occur to me that it might add any extra effort, and it hasn't. There were certain times on the journey that two legs would have come in handy, but as it is, I only have one, so I don't wish for more."

"How long ago did you lose it?"

Kyle thought and responded, "I was hand-propping an aircraft with a starter issue about eight years ago. The other mechanic and I were working to repair the engine. The aircraft leaked some oil on the pavement, and I went off balance and into the propeller when I tried to start it. When I left the shop about a year ago, I was working explaining the service their aircraft needed to customers and writing up repairs." Then, pointing to his prosthetic leg, he said, "Obviously, they didn't want this thing around the aircraft, so I wasn't working on airplanes anymore."

James raised his eyebrows, "What's hand-propping? Clearly, it's dangerous."

"If it's done safely, there's no danger," Kyle smirked and shrugged, "but that would include good footing. Hand-propping is basically spinning the propeller by hand to get the engine going. That's how it was always done before aircraft had electrical systems." He lowered his voice, "The one we were working on just had a dead battery, but the shop wanted that job finished as soon as we could get it done."

"Wow! Many people never get back on track after a loss like that, but you've done what those people think is too difficult. How do you think you did it?"

Kyle said, "Maybe it was because I had to overcome many difficulties years before, and that could have set me up to understand how massive the challenge might seem when in truth, they're insignificant. All too often, the events that really impact our lives go unnoticed."

James nodded, saying, "So true." With a smile and pointing to his cup, he added, "I didn't realize this coffee came with a philosophy lesson. How long are you guys going to be in town? I'd love for you to stay at my place."

"We weren't really planning to be here very long, but we'd love to stay with you while we're here." Kyle looked at his coffee. "I'm going back in to get a refill. Can I get you one?"

James handed his empty cup to Kyle with a nod and a smile. Pointing at Dingo, "I'll watch your pooch."

Once inside, Kyle spotted a notice about the local bookstore's event in a few days. It was a book sale and author signing. The author wrote one of the books Kyle read before his trek. Since they're staying in town for a bit, he and Dingo could rest up before the book signing. Also, it would give them an excellent chance to look at these mountains from the eastern side.

Although standing in line for coffee might seem like an odd place to have an epiphany, some might think walking a thousand miles is also odd. Kyle understood that being courageous enough to ask the question is all that's required to bring a response. Maybe he'd been afraid to ask because he knew some action would be required, like taking a step when he received a response or creating a silent place to ask the question. The internal silence was the most challenging portion for him to do so he could hear the answer. The answers were always with him, but the answers might come in a disagreeable form. Kyle could only assume he'd missed many other answers because he knew some objectionable action might be required. He needed a teacher to point out these things and remembered the statement, "When the student is ready, the teacher will appear." *Maybe I wasn't ready before. Perhaps Dingo is preparing me for the teacher, or maybe she is the teacher.* It seemed that walking many miles was helping make him ready and put things in perspective. He'd read that one person held all the answers; that one was Kyle. All he had to do was be courageous enough to ask the question and then listen for the reply. He thought back to the sticker that said, "Dog is my copilot," and grinned.

Kyle got to the head of the line with a smile still on his face and refilled the coffees. He walked out in the morning light with coffee to join James and Dingo. James was sitting in partial shade so he could rest a hand on Dingo. Kyle sat down and offered the other dog treat to Dingo. She swiftly accepted it as Kyle turned to ask James about this town named after a rock. "How long have you lived in this town?"

"I moved here about five years ago. I really like this town." Pointing at Kyle for emphasis, "You should visit the history museum. It's a fascinating town, and the museum will give you all the facts. I've got a map at home to give you good directions."

"That might be a great way to show myself around. I might do that today if you don't mind me leaving Dingo at your place."

"Not at all. We'll get along great."

Kyle left Dingo napping at James' house again a few days later when he walked to the bookstore for the book signing. Kyle arrived early to spend some time reading books in the store. He didn't bring his copy of the yellow book with him as he had traded it somewhere in California. One of the bookstore employees approached him mid-way down an aisle. "Can I help you find something?"

"I'm just browsing. Really, I'm here for the signing."

Sara said, "The signing should start in about an hour." Shifting her gaze to the book in his hands, "That is one of my favorites."

Kyle looked down and seemed to see the book he was holding for the first time. The cover showed a woman facing away from the observer. Sara pointed at the book and told him, "If you haven't read that one, you should."

"I've read something else by the same author, but not this. A friend gave me that copy, and the book seemed to be about discovering and following your destiny."

"The one you're talking about is fascinating." She pointed again to the book in his hands and said, "If you liked that one, you'd certainly like this one."

With that, he tucked this new book under his arm and asked Sara, "What else is a good read?"

Sara asked, "What do you generally like to read?"

Kyle shrugged his shoulders. "It's kinda difficult to say just because lately I've been reading very different books than I used to."

"I understand. Follow me." She walked farther down the aisle and scanned the books. "There it is! This is another one of my favorites." She handed Kyle a dark blue book with a circle-shaped web design on the cover. Kyle thought the 2-dimensional circle on the cover continued around the back to make a complete sphere. Holding it out, he said, "I'll let you know what I think." As Kyle turned it around to see if he was right about the sphere, he found there was just writing on the back. Kyle thought with a smile that he now had two books to read while he stayed with James. Kyle thanked Sara for her help, took the two books to the counter to pay, and found a comfortable spot to begin reading. When the signing started, he'd read about a chapter of the blue book. He placed a mark in his book so he could join the gathering.

The author started the signing by greeting the crowd gathered to hear her speak, saying, "My name's Jen." In that bookstore, were crammed about 70 people designed for maybe 30. Sara found an empty spot next to Kyle.

While Jen was signing her books, she said, "Thanks for coming out." She looked at the crowd, saying, "I'm always curious to find out what prompted you all to come out, and it's always a great opportunity for me to learn more about my readers."

Someone in the group said, "I feel like I'm at a crossroads, and I don't know how to proceed." Many people murmured yeah and nodded to convey they were in a similar situation.

Jen said, "That's awesome because much of my book is devoted to that idea. Waiting for a perfect moment to take action might never happen, and you have to know it's okay to make mistakes. Sometimes that first step seems impossible for people, but it's not. You gotta just take a step to show yourself it's doable."

Kyle raised his eyebrows, thinking, *Is this author related to that Swami who could almost read my mind? Reading her book, I realized I was allowing my friends to define the borders of my identity and had to take that step to discover me and push through all that added anxiety from their questioning.*

Looking around, *All these other people brought their copy of the yellow book to have it signed, but I don't have my copy, so I'll just wait to get a minute with the author.* The line passed by where Sara was standing, and she asked if he had a copy he was reading. "I don't. I read it and traded it for another book a few months ago." A couple of minutes later, Kyle was at the head of the line and asked again for his copy by the author. He told Jen, "I don't have it. After I read it, I traded it for another book in California, but the words you wrote made my journey okay to take when so many tried to talk me out of it, telling me I was about to make a huge mistake."

Jen joked. "I hope you got a good book in trade."

Kyle smiled. "Of course I did! It was an awesome one."

Jen asked, "A moment ago, you said journey. What journey did you take?"

"I'm still on it, I think." Kyle briefly explained how hard it was to leave his hometown. Jen turned to address the crowd, saying, "This is precisely what I was talking about in my book; just taking a step. "You may not know where it's going or why you're taking that step, but movement produces more movement, and eventually, you have momentum carrying you in the direction of your dreams! You're allowed not to know what you're doing when you set out, but trust me, you will figure it out, and you may get inspired by something else too."

Kyle turned to make room for the next person in line, but Jen said, "Wait a sec. I want you to have a copy of my new book, so I have something to sign for you. My email is in the back, so maybe you can update me on your travels." Jen signed her new book and scribbled something else in the back. Handing it to Kyle, saying, "Safe journey."

Kyle smiled at Jen, "Thanks so much."

Jen chuckled, "And I hope you get another awesome book in trade for this one. I look forward to hearing from you."

Kyle smiled and walked back. He held the book out to Sara. "You've probably already seen her new book."

Sara grinned. "Yes, but not one that's signed. Would you like to have coffee in the morning?"

"I'd absolutely love to. Dingo loves those little bagel dog treats at the coffee shop right around the corner."

Sara smiled at that. "I'm guessin' Dingo, is your dog? How about we meet at about 7?" Kyle nodded and said they would see her at the coffee shop. Sara turned back to help a customer.

As they approached the following day, Sara waved from the table Kyle had occupied a few days before. Kyle left Dingo with Sara at the table and asked, "Can I bring you anything from inside?"

Sara said, "I've already got coffee, but don't forget the treats for Dingo!" When Kyle came out with his coffee and bagel, he had a couple of treats for Dingo.

Kyle told Sara he'd read half the book with the web circle on the cover, and the question he kept coming up with was, "Who is this person called Kyle if not the beliefs that I have?"

Sara replied with a smile. Nodding, she said, "I always question beliefs that come up for me. I think It helps me discover who I am. If you just inherited some beliefs, then those are not you. So many of the things we do are just something we mimic. Maybe we saw it on T.V., or our parents showed us, and then we just started doing and believing it."

Kyle thought *This seems to be the essence of evolution that came to me in that ghost town. Nobody can evolve by using inherited beliefs, and I remember thinking that evolution might only occur if one knows who they are and then decides who they aspire to be.*

Kyle realized that he didn't have a clue about who he might be and invited Sara into that idea with, "Do you think one could evolve without having all those beliefs?" Kyle blew the steam from the top of his espresso, saying, "I guess I'm wondering if we can't skip all that self-knowledge while we move on?"

"It seems that knowing what is essentially you would be a crucial part of moving on and evolving." Sara leaned to pet Dingo saying, "I wonder how anyone could evolve without having some self-knowledge. If I tried to evolve into the best me using what someone else told me, what they think is me, I don't think I'd evolve too far."

Kyle nodded, saying, "I'm sure that's right. I like that other book that I got from you at the bookstore. I was reading a little of it last night too. It seems the girl chose a path that could be very difficult and unique. I guess many people avoid anything that might be difficult or unique."

Sara replied, "I think so too, and I'm glad you like that one. The girl in that book chose a difficult path that revealed her authentic identity. It was inspiring because she picked a unique path. Choosing a unique path is pretty easy, but the difficult part is taking that first step like Jen was talking about at the signing."

Sara looked at her watch and said, "Speaking of that, it's about time for me to unlock the doors to the bookstore. I do lunch at about 12:30. Join me so we can keep talking."

Kyle told her, "That'd be great. I'd love to hear your thoughts on some of the other books I've read. I'll see you this afternoon, then."

Kyle left Dingo at the bookstore door at about 12:15 to browse a bit before meeting Sara for lunch. He started down the aisle under the sign that read Eastern philosophy. Reading each title, ambling slowly in front of the bookshelf, his fingers gliding over the spine of each book: Kyle stopped when he reached a small blue novel and slid the book out to read the back. He'd heard of this person before and his gentle way of directing attention back to the individual that might be searching for knowledge. *I know the saying, 'Searching leads to searching,' but this book might have some other clues.*

Kyle brought this new book to the register, and Sara's last sale before lunch was Kyle's new book. She pointed to the book and said, "I've not read that one, but I've heard he was a great philosopher. How many books are you reading now?"

Kyle held up three fingers.

Sara smirked, nodded, and said, "I get it! There's a place I like around the corner for lunch. Let me get someone to cover the cash register."

Kyle waited by the door while she changed places with another worker, and in a few moments, Sara was warmly greeted by Dingo waiting outside, and the three were walking down the street. Kyle turned to Sara, asking, "Have you read any Buddhist authors?"

"Some. It seems that all the masters in the books used words to point to the truth. I think the unity of their message was truth, or the wisdom to see truth. Some masters were concerned with describing the truth they saw from a particular viewpoint or with some knowledge. But, I think they knew the words themselves are rather worthless and just knowledge. Some readers become infatuated with the words and never look to the truth the words would point at." Sara shrugged as if to emphasize she had said something insignificant and probably common knowledge and, pointing to some sunshades hanging over tables, said, "This is the restaurant."

Pointing out the water dish to Dingo, Kyle sat at a table for two. "Are you saying we shouldn't read books?"

Sara looked over the menu at Kyle with raised eyebrows to exclaim, "Not at all! Books have a critical message and help us to look toward the truth. The bookstore I work in is filled with books that are, in turn, filled with words. They help to remind me that the truth is always available. It may be truth could be found in the pause between the words." Shrugging again and lifting the menu to read, she said, "I don't mean to make it sound mystical or difficult to find because it's not at all. It's as easy as making a cup of tea, and anyone can do it."

The waiter interrupted briefly to take their order.

Kyle pointed to Dingo, "So many times I deliberate on some mystical, philosophical idea, and I'm completely astonished when I turn my attention to Dingo and see her acting out that very idea. I think she understands these ideas that I struggle with."

Sara said, "I'm struck by that same thought often." Pointing at Dingo, Sara continued, "Somehow, these non-human beings have an understanding of ideas that we think are deeply philosophical and difficult to comprehend. I think they're probably just the ancient masters in a different form." Smiling, Sara added, "Dingo could be Paramahansa Yogananda or Lao Tzu. Any master would probably tell you it's not difficult to achieve wisdom. Words are often misleading on the path to truth. I think the biggest obstacle for humans seeking wisdom is discovering a sense of peace or finding that pause between words. Pointing to Dingo, "It seems the animals, having already discovered that pause, spend their whole lives just pointing to the truth from silence. They never make an exhibition of wisdom; they just quietly point. It seems they couldn't care less If nobody looks because they know the truth is there.

The different traditions all have what they might think is a distinctive word, but all the different traditions point to the same thing. The word emptiness is a great example. People tend to look for what they have learned the word means, but that's just a logical search, and the actual feeling the individual gets makes them think they must be on the wrong path. From fear, they might move away from the true feeling of emptiness and try to, instead, fill that space with events or something else to not feel empty. That's just a block to keep out the silence," Sara looked up from her menu at Kyle, "which is just another word for emptiness. I was often confused by all the available knowledge, thinking my life would be much better with different knowledge or events. However, I noticed that all the ancient masters I studied had something in common with Dingo here." Sara pointed at the sleeping form of Dingo.

Kyle whispered, "What was that?"

"I think they all have the ability to welcome silence and fill themselves with it. They never shield themselves from it and even seek more space to accommodate silence; sometimes, they'd expel knowledge to gain more space."

Kyle said, "In my reading of some of the masters, I didn't hear much about the connection between wisdom, grace, breath, and truth, but I've found they're all one."

"I think they are. All the masters point to the same thing, and what I was saying about different words sometimes being misleading because they might simply be using a different word to talk about truth, wisdom, or grace."

Their meals were served, and both became quiet.

That night Kyle relaxed by writing in his journal.

I recall Lucy saying something about trusting the tools always to be available, so I think it must be the same with seeing wisdom. The most challenging thing for most people (and me!) is trusting wisdom to be present at all times. Finding wisdom is as easy as creating a quiet place, and all I have to do is look at Dingo to see how simple that is. In fact, all dogs I've seen share this innate quality. I used to believe I could pry wisdom from an experience like prying a gold nugget from a rock. When Lucy mentioned trusting tools, I automatically had a notion of hammers, wrenches, and pliers; but trusting those 'tools' is not what Lucy was talking about. I now realize her using the word 'tools' was simply a metaphor, and the only tool that will stimulate wisdom is silence. My time around this dog has been immensely valuable in my attainment of wisdom because she constantly shows me the only 'tool' that will work. This dog is intimately familiar with and always points to the tool of silence.

silence of the dog

wisdom realized

The following day, the pair met Sara at their favorite shop for coffee. Kyle asked, "Sara, you seem lost in thought. Why?"

"I feel like it's time for me to go in a more creative direction, but I don't know which way to go."

Kyle tilted his head. "What do you mean?"

"I've been thinking of producing something authentic, something just from me, like a gift. A gift seems only meaningful when it's authentic; you put yourself fully into it and then give it away without a thought of return. I don't think the gift matters, but if it is an authentic expression, it'll always be awesome. I'm not sure what my expression will be, but I know it'll be something creative like painting or writing. I like to think of being creative as kinda like making a query that goes out to the universe, and a statement can then come back in the form of a written word, a sketch, a painting, or whatever. Creation is like wisdom in movement."

"Like grace?"

Sara paused to look at Dingo and said, "Yeah, wisdom in motion would be graceful!"

"You've read so many books; maybe it is time to write one." Kyle paused for a moment and said, "Maybe I can help. I love to draw; I could illustrate for you."

Sara threw her head back and exclaimed, "That'd be great. I'd love to have your help. How long are you planning to stay in town?"

Kyle paused to look at the silent mountains he and Dingo had crossed a week before. "I like being in this town." Looking under the table at Dingo and reaching to run a hand over the dozing form of Dingo. "What do you think if we stayed here for a bit?" Turning to Sara, "Well, that settles it. I think we'll be here for the foreseeable future.

That night back at James's, Kyle saw his journal on the table and continued writing after his last entry.

I had never thought about creation as wisdom in motion or simply grace. The home I was longing for and seeking was always with me: I just had to make use of my creativity to know that home was always in me. I realize the most challenging step for me to take has been to move into the creator that I am and always have been. Allowing the emptiness to be within me was the first step in creating. I see I distracted myself from noticing emptiness by filling my head with useless trivial facts. I'm sure at the time, it must have seemed entirely relevant to find out how old a Saguaro cactus might get to be or some other insignificant fact, but it seems like that information would be a distraction for the mind or like filling up on empty calories.

12 You are the key

Kyle clip-clopped up the sidewalk to the house he and Sara rented a few months ago. Dingo welcomed him at the door to tell him it was past her feeding time. Kyle obediently followed her to the kitchen, placing a scoop of food in her dish. He remained for the twenty seconds it would take her to gobble her food and see her customary play bow. Kyle accepted the bow gratefully as he looked around the kitchen and crouched to pet Dingo. He felt enormous gratitude for finding a destination for them both and knew this was not a finish line but more of a fantastic resting spot.

He recalled with affection the many miles they had traveled together and all the friends they made along the way. Many people feel more comfortable conversing with a stranger when a dog accompanies them. Most importantly, though, with her help, Kyle learned the master was always with him, just waiting to be discovered. The anxiety had come from ignoring the master within and only following his thoughts. He remembered with a smile about the bumper sticker they saw a long time ago that read, "Dog is my co-pilot," and pondered his gratefulness towards this 'co-pilot' that helped make his journey a success.

Sara and Kyle wrote children's books about a dog named Dingo. Those books would be filled with the wisdom that a dog helps expose. Kyle paused by the office door where the newest "Dingo" book was being created. Kyle looked at the most recent illustration for the book and thought *Sara is quite the storyteller. It's sometimes a challenge to develop an image that follows her storyline, but I know it's inside me, just waiting for me to discover.* He continued to the living room bookshelf to shelve the book he had just finished about travel in India for Sara.

He found the journal he used during his travels on the bookshelf and wrote after reading a few entries.

Someone told me long ago that humans are the only species that knows they are going to die. At the time, it made perfect sense, but now I think other species see the cycle and don't spend their whole lives in fear of what comes next or trying to hide from the truth. There are so many things we don't know, and I thank Dingo for being my guide to show me that. I see that Dingo connected with the ancient master in me, and we all come from the same source—the ancient master in her, connected with the ancient master in me. We, humans have ancient wisdom that has been covered with years of messages saying something is lacking within, but the correct message is always discovered by the ancient master within.

master is within

challenging you to become

you beyond you

This morning I heard someone call my name just before I woke. It was in that moment between waking and sleeping: so it wasn't a dream, and it

couldn't have been my conscious mind. Am I close to some point I was navigating toward? I don't know, but maybe that was me, talking to me, or perhaps it was my ancient master. I know the ancient master can hear the message from anything because they know the art of listening. A whisper almost not heard or a mountain that seems to make no sound is sensed by the master. My biggest challenge was accepting that I was the same as the master. The master holds no extraordinary powers or unique talents. I've often heard that only the chosen have talents, but I no longer have that particular anxiety or belief.

Eddie is coming to visit in a few weeks. It'll be great to see an old friend because it seems that everyone I know now I only met very recently on my journey.

Kyle met Eddie at the airport a few days later and showed him back to his house. As they walked up the stairs, Kyle told Eddie, "Sara will be back around six."

Eddie made himself comfortable in Kyle's new cushy recliner and, turning to Kyle, said, "Tell me everything that happened after you left Portland. I got that postcard from you; I think you were somewhere in Utah. How's your brother?"

Kyle nodded in agreement to being in Utah and said, "Daniel is doing great. He's a happy dad with two children."

"Isn't he a few years older than you? Didn't he start a family about 20 years ago? Isn't he a little too old to be doing another family?"

Kyle shrugged, "Maybe, but each person can decide what tools they use to evolve."

Eddie shook his head in confusion and asked, "Evolve? What do you mean, evolve?"

"There is a theory we may learn in this lifetime and then take that information into the next lifetime. So, we might choose the best tools to bring us lessons in this lifetime and help us evolve into the next one. I think the biggest hurdle for most in the evolution process, me included, is discovering and embracing our own emptiness. It seems that people will do anything to avoid recognizing their emptiness. Maybe if their next step is discovering emptiness, they may face many distractions. For me, every time I went to look at where emptiness might be, some distraction jumped out at me that I thought couldn't wait."

Eddie furrowed his brow so hard that he made one eye-brow out of two and said, "I love to listen to you talk, though I usually don't understand a thing you say. Maybe you're just a convoluted thinker, but I hope that makes you a better seeker."

Kyle smiled, saying, "I hope that makes me a better _finder_! In my experience, seeking just seems to lead to more seeking.

Eddie chuckled at that, saying, "I haven't the faintest clue what that means, but I know I'm seeking a beer right now! Is there a pub around here?"

Kyle said, "Sure. It's about a twenty-minute walk from here." Pointing to the south, he continued, "That way. Come on, let's go.

"Cool. It'll be good to stretch my legs after being cramped in that airplane."

Walking down the stairs of the house, Kyle told Eddie, "I am perfectly content that my insights might seem like sheer foolishness. My insights are merely my insights, and I know they might not make any sense to other people."

Eddie asked, "Do you think those _insights_ are from your journey?"

"Sort of, but I think my journey brought a lot of insights, and one is allowing me to be okay with the fact that it's all right to see things the way I see them. I see things differently, and that's simply how I see them."

Kyle turned to look back at Eddie. "You know, it's funny _thinking_ should come into our conversation 'cause I always thought I could think my way through anything, but a very wise person clued me into the fact that thinking just leads back to itself. Kind of like seeking leading back to seeking; thinking can never uncover truth and simply leads to more thinking. People try to solve problems with thinking but end up inserting some random answer where the truth would go. Those same people usually decide they have thought about the issue enough and pacify themselves with the idea that they've thought it through thoroughly. Any further investigation or possible truth-finding is simply lost."

Eddie sputtered, "Truth?! How can you possibly solve any problem without thinking?"

Kyle said, "Thinking is an awesome tool for working out some algebraic equation, but can't even get close to truth. It seems that all the ancient masters pointed at different aspects of the same truth. Jesus, Buddha, and Krishnamurti were all pointing at truth. They experienced truth but maybe couldn't relay truth to us with words, so they pointed. Utilizing flexible thinking or using thought only where it functions seems critical to experience the pause between the question and the answer where the truth resides."

Eddie said, "I can't even imagine what you might mean."

He remembered a book in John's house and described part of it for Eddie. "I saw this image of a finger pointing at the moon in a book I borrowed from a friend. Maybe it was Jesus, it doesn't matter who it was, and I didn't understand it then, but now I get it! Most people only think about the finger or the person pointing but never even consider where the finger may point. The truth the finger points to, or the moon in that image, gets lost because of thought. Thinking tends to draw one's attention away from truth. Fortunately, I had Dingo constantly pointing to the truth."

"So, are you saying that Dingo is like Jesus?"

Kyle smiled broadly and chuckled. "Maybe she is, but I'm really saying that everything communicates in a language we may not immediately understand or see because of thinking. Communication is always just another finger-pointing to the moon. Remember when we sat next to that river back home? It probably sounded like a babbling brook, but the river had a different language. It's kinda like hearing Japanese when you don't understand the language; you wouldn't assume there's no information there. With a different language, you know it's another language, and people use it to communicate information. That river was speaking, but I was too focused on being hungry or whatever to hear the information there."

Eddie laughed, saying, "Let me get this straight: You think your dog is Jesus, and water talks to you. Should I be concerned for your mental health? Maybe you want me to call a doctor?"

Kyle laughed and, through his smile, said, "That's funny! No, you don't need to call anyone. I'm just saying that a dog or a river could have some vital information, and it just uses a different language." Kyle stopped to pick up a stone on the sidewalk and handed it to Eddie. "Take that stone, for example. Everything communicates. That stone reminds me of a crystal hanging in my kitchen window. The kitchen is filled with a thousand tiny shafts of light when the sun hits the crystal. It's a wonderful sight, all those little rainbows on the refrigerator and the counters."

Eddie held out the stone when he asked Kyle, "So this stone reminds you of a crystal you have at home? That crystal may be kinda unique, but there are millions of flat gray stones like this one."

Kyle looked at the stone, saying, "Exactly." He waved a hand, indicating everything around, "Millions of subtle voices," Kyle pointed skyward, "all pointing."

Pointing at the stone in Eddie's hand, Kyle said, "That stone may not make a sound like a river, *but there is a sound.* My crystal communicates through a stunning light show, the river through that babbling sound, and that stone through its subtle sound."

Eddie smiled and shook his head. "Kyle, I have no idea what you're trying to say, I'm just happy to see you, and I hope you had a good journey." Pointing back at nothing but the way they'd come, "And you think Dingo showed you that?"

Kyle smiled broadly again. "I'm having a great journey, and I'm delighted to see you too." Kyle turned his palms up like he was holding a fragile gift, saying, "I know when I try to explain my insights, it may come out sounding like gibberish, and often, it doesn't even resemble the thing I'm trying to describe. I've gotten okay with that, and maybe Dingo did assist me by pointing, but I guess it was finally me that did the looking."

Kyle stopped walking and turned to Eddie, "We humans toot our horns and shout from roof-tops 'Look at all the advances in technology or any other marvels of our society,' but I say the significant things we can't do, and I see the dogs doing them with absolute ease. What's more, things dogs do are always infused with grace. We struggle to do unconditional love for fifteen minutes, yet dogs do that for fifteen years straight, so shouldn't we at least look in the direction our co-pilot points?" He glanced up the way they'd come from, "I know my journey, so far, maybe didn't make any sense; me leaving relative comfort to go look behind trees and under rocks searching for emptiness," Kyle gripped Eddie's elbow, "so thanks for being around and listening."

13 Full circle

Kyle's favorite trail for walking Dingo was a path through the forest a few blocks away from the house, and after stopping at the coffee shop for his bagel and Dingo's treats, the pair continued to the trailhead. As there were a couple of cars parked near the trail, Kyle assumed they'd meet some other hikers, but as they started up the trail, Kyle noticed the forest was so strangely quiet that he paused every few yards to look around for some sign of life: A bird or squirrel, anything that might make some noise. Kyle gazed up through the branches of the ponderosas around and lingered at all the clearings to look out across the green clumps of trees.

Kyle watched Dingo trot up the trail through shafts of sunlight and patches of shade. She paused at a bend in the trail to gaze out across miles of trees. Kyle noticed her body posture change after a few quiet moments and remembered when they were visiting Lucy and Stella; Dingo paused her digging in the beach to stare out over the ocean and sensed it was time to continue. She became slightly rigid, like she was a bit electrified, but he knew it was some sound. Kyle remembered wishing he could hear that sound too, but now he knows the subtle sound is different for everyone. Kyle smiled to himself at this understanding and reached out to touch the nearest tree. Dingo looked back down the path at him, and Kyle thought he saw her nod. Shocked, Kyle looked more intensely at her for some further sign, but Dingo just turned and continued trotting up the trail.

Kyle looked up through the branches at the intense blue sky and immediately understood that Dingo's message was to move on alone. Kyle's shoulders slumped at this solemn information, and he muttered, "Really?" A hand went to his throat as a quiet sob trickled out, and he whispered disappointedly, "Dingo?" as she trotted out of sight. He glanced back down the trail, sadly looking at the six footprints they left in the dirt, thinking he'd probably never see Dingo again. Kyle wandered up the path, leaving just two prints now. He stopped near the clearing where Dingo received her message and turned to look over the green forest valley to the next hill. Resting with his back against a tree, he slid gloomily down to sit next to the trail.

Glancing sadly up the path in the direction Dingo had gone thinking, *I'll probably not see her again, but I feel like it was an extraordinary gift for her to have chosen me to travel with.* Kyle gazed across the green valley at the tree-covered hills miles away, *Dingo perhaps found me on purpose just to share grace with me and to show me I possessed it too. I'll be infinitely grateful for her constant displays of wisdom. I thought people were teaching me and sharing wisdom, but I'll be forever indebted to Dingo, persistently gifting me with the fact that wisdom isn't only kept by humans.* Kyle pointed up the trail to the bend where he'd last seen Dingo and gently placed that finger on his chest. Gently tapping his chest, *I can honor the gift she gave me.*

When he felt like he was ready to go, he reached above his head for a branch to grab so he could pull himself up. Kyle didn't feel the bark on the branch; in fact, the branch felt soft in his hand. He looked up at the branch, and Kyle discovered it was an arm that belonged to his friend Eddie. Eddie was reaching out to help him sit up in bed. Confused, Kyle asked Eddie, "Where's Dingo?"

Eddie furrowed his brow, "Who's Dingo?"

Made in the USA
Columbia, SC
29 April 2024